THE SURGEON'S DAUGHTER

THE SURGEON

After almost running
sister down, Jenna was
arrogant stranger had t
the near-accident had been h
was even more annoyed when
father brought his new surgi
home for dinner—and he tu
to be the obnoxious stranger
was a competent nurse but so
the disturbingly attractive registrar had
a knack for catching her at a disadvantage.
Then one terrible night, Jenna's father was
attacked by a knife-wielding gang—the
leader of which was an old boyfriend of
Jenna's ...

The Surgeon's Daughter

by
Priscilla Page

Dales Large Print Books
Long Preston, North Yorkshire,
England.

British Library Cataloguing in Publication Data.

Page, Priscilla
 The surgeon's daughter.

 A catalogue record for this book is
 available from the British Library

 ISBN 1-85389-939-9 pbk

First published in Great Britain by Robert Hale Ltd., 1991

Cover illustration © Heslop by arrangement with Allied Artists

Published in Large Print 1999 by arrangement with Robert Hale Ltd.

Dales Large Print is an imprint of
Library Magna Books Ltd.
Printed and bound in Great Britain by
T.J. International Ltd., Cornwall, PL28 8RW.

One

'Is that how you stop the traffic, push the child into the middle of the road?' The deep blue eyes staring down into Jenna's were blazing with fury and contempt.

'I ... I ...' Jenna stuttered, her whole body shaking, her grip on the baby-buggy tightening with shock. One moment she had checked the road before crossing with her little sister Annie, the next she was jumping back onto the pavement desperately pulling back the baby-buggy.

'You ... You ... what?' taunted the towering, angry man, his mouth drawn thin and hard with the strength of his rage. He caught hold of her arm impatiently, as she fought to control her trembling.

'It's lucky,' he said tersely, 'I noticed you standing by the road. I didn't dream you would start to cross just as I accelerated away from the kerb. As it was I only just managed to stop in time.'

Jenna looked at the MG, it was only inches away from the baby-buggy. Her face was white and stricken, her teeth were chattering and the velvet-brown eyes were fixed and wide.

'Come on, you'd better sit down,' he decreed. 'Come into the coffee-shop, that's best.'

Taking the buggy in one hand and holding firmly onto the girl with the other he pushed open the swing doors of Rossi's coffee-shop and sat her down at the nearest table. Two-year-old Annie sat straight up in her chair, looking at Jenna's stricken face, and pronounced censoriously: 'Bad man!' Her accusing eyes were turned on the stranger.

People at surrounding tables turned and stared, but he ignored them.

'Two coffees and an orange,' he said to the hovering waiter. 'Black or white?'

he asked Jenna who nodded, unable to speak. He sat down and took hold of her wrist. The pulse was racing still. He examined her with his eyes. She gazed back defiantly, her brown eyes large against the white skin. Her long unruly hair fell in dark, curly tendrils about her face as it escaped from its restraining band. A tear trembled on an eyelash and she dashed it away angrily.

'I'm fine!' The panic and fear for Annie were subsiding now, and Jenna straightened her small frame and lifted a defiant chin. Snatching her arm away she busied herself with settling Annie, taking her coat, putting a paper napkin in the neck of the child's dress and handing her the orange-juice.

The resemblance between Jenna and the child was striking. Annie's hair was fairer, but both had the same bone-structure and dark, almost black eyes, though Jenna was twenty and the child only two.

'Drink your coffee,' he ordered in a peremptory tone and picking up his own cup in strong, capable-looking fingers, took a deep draught.

Obediently Jenna drank, managing to stop her teeth from chattering against the cup.

'My name is Tom Yorke. I have recently moved to Darnton. And you?'

Fleetingly Jenna reflected on the slight West Country accent in the deep voice. 'Jenna er ... Jane Neville,' she replied briefly and was surprised at how normal her voice sounded in her own ears, 'and this is Annie.' Her eyes softened as she looked at the child who was making a great noise out of drinking the orange-juice.

Tom's face changed. 'And Annie very nearly wasn't!' He spoke harshly. 'Perhaps you will be more careful another time with your child's life.' Nodding brusquely he strode out of the coffee-shop without a backward glance, leaving Jenna seething with rage this time rather than fright.

How could he think she would take chances with Annie's life? In her opinion, he was as much to blame as she was for the near accident.

The rosy colour came and went in her cheeks as she stared out of the window at the tall, fair man getting into the sports car. And how could he have thought she was Annie's mother? Her thoughts ran hotly as she finished her coffee. The arrogant, imperious so-and-so! He should have stayed where he came from if he didn't know how to treat people. Wiping Annie's chin with the napkin and bundling her into her coat, she left the cafe and turned for home.

Jenna lived with her father and step-mother in a large, old, stone house on the outskirts of Darnton, a typical north-eastern market-town. Her mother had died when Jenna was ten. As she walked home pushing Annie, who had now fallen asleep with the motion of the buggy, she put all thoughts of the odious Mr Yorke out of her mind. She concentrated on the pleasant afternoon she had planned, looking forward to a long lazy afternoon in the garden followed by a leisurely bath and shampoo before dinner.

Jenna's days off were precious to her, a respite from the hard work of the wards at the busy general hospital where she was a student nurse. She still was not used to seeing the pain of some of the patients and found it hard to control her feelings. Yet she loved the work at the busy district hospital which served a large rural area as well as the town. She loved the camaraderie of the staff, the feeling of satisfaction when a patient went home fit and well.

Now, humming softly to herself, Jenna turned into the drive as the front door opened and Pam, her stepmother, emerged.

'Hi, Jenna! Has she been a good girl?' She lowered her voice as she saw the child was sleeping. 'Oh dear, that means she won't sleep this afternoon, and I did specially want to go to cookery class today. Do you mind looking after her, Jenna?'

Pam, who looked not much older than Jenna though in fact she was thirty, looked out of sandy lashes at her step-daughter. She was a sunny-natured woman with laughter-lines around her mouth, which showed when she grinned, which she did now. She knew she could rely on Jenna.

Jenna sighed ruefully. So much for a long lazy afternoon on the lawn; some chance with a lively two-year-old newly awakened from sleep.

'Oh, go on then, I'll give Annie her lunch when she wakes.' She grinned back at Pam who laughed comfortably.

'Well, if you're sure!' With a cheery wave Pam fairly danced down the path.

'We all know you could do with the lessons!' was Jenna's parting sally after the swiftly retreating form. Pam was renowned for her abysmal efforts in the kitchen where she usually attempted something far too complicated for a poor cook. Which didn't seem to bother her a bit, her long-suffering family having to sample the results.

Looking up from easing the buggy through the door whilst trying not to wake Annie, Jenna saw Pam running back and gave her an enquiring glance. Pam spoke while hurrying up the path, ready to run straight back out.

'Oh, Jenna, I forgot, your father phoned, he's bringing the new registrar home for dinner; you wouldn't be an angel and pick the salad stuffs for me? And wash them, please?' Not waiting for an answer she went on her way.

Jenna groaned; the way things were going she would be lucky to get any time to herself. Her father, a consultant surgeon, was as gregarious as his wife and loved nothing better than to bring company home, despite the hazards of Pam's cooking.

At a quarter to eight that evening Jenna was just about ready to go downstairs to greet her father's guest. The salads were freshly made and awaiting the dressing, the steaks were buttered and under the grill ready to cook, and the pavlova Pam had brought home in triumph from cookery class was only slightly burned around the edges.

Jenna's hair was piled up in a shining mass on top of her head, the curls controlled by Spanish combs, and her slight figure was encased in a slinky, grey silk dress which had cost a month's salary. She stared into the glass thoughtfully, and decided she needed a touch of colour on her cheeks and lips, though normally she bothered little with make-up. But then, when out of uniform she usually wore jeans or cotton dresses; the slinky grey number had been a sudden whim on her part.

Applying the lip-rouge she wondered absently about the new registrar, not so much was he attractive, but was he easy to work with, or rather for. Jenna was very conscious that being her father's daughter often made her seniors expect more of her than the other students.

Pulling a face at her reflection she bent and pulled on strappy sandals with ridiculously high heels. Sometimes she got fed up with the sensible though comfortable shoes required for ward work. When she saw these in Brown's on the High Street, the exact shade of her dress, she succumbed. Closing her bedroom door quietly to avoid waking Annie, newly bathed and sleeping peacefully in the next room, she started downstairs.

Jenna halted in her tracks, almost falling over as she turned her ankle over slightly in the moment of surprise; she stumbled and had to grab the banister with both hands to steady herself.

'Are you all right, darling?' Jenna barely heard her father as he started forward from where he was greeting a tall, fair-haired young man, a man becoming all too familiar.

'Yes, yes, thanks Daddy, it was nothing.' Descending the last few stairs she held out her hand to the guest in what she hoped was a nonchalant fashion.

'You two have already met?' asked her father with a quizzical expression; he obviously had noted the rising colour in Jenna's face and the slightly amused expression on Tom's.

Looking at David Neville's face it was easy to see where both his daughters got their dark eyes and curling hair. There was a marked family resemblance even though the father's hair was streaked with grey. At fifty he was still a pleasant, good-looking man with nice eyes and mouth; he was adored by his young wife and family.

'We met in the High Street, sir. Or perhaps I should say we bumped into each other.' Tom smiled sardonically at Jenna.

'Oh,' said a slightly mystified Mr Neville, glancing at his daughter, who by now had recovered her equilibrium. He seemed about to pursue the matter but just then Pam appeared from the kitchen.

'Hello, David,' she grinned cheerfully as she kissed him on the cheek then turned to greet their guest without waiting for an introduction.

'This must be Dr Yorke,' she said. 'I'm David's wife, Pam; how do you do? Dinner won't be long.' She took a step back towards the kitchen door. 'Pour the sherry, will you, David? I'll just go and turn on the grill.'

'Yes,' said David. 'Well, shall we go into the lounge?' Tom politely indicated to Jenna to precede him, his gaze enigmatic as he took in the slinky dress and make-up. The lounge was a pleasant room, bearing the stamp of Pam's personality, home-loving though untidy. Cheerful cretonne-covered chairs and sofa were placed on a parquet floor reflecting the light from the floor-length windows open to the flower-garden. The effect was bright and airy, enhanced by cream-washed walls on which hung a couple of oilscapes of Teesdale.

David poured the sherry at the sideboard.

'Sherry for you, Tom?' he asked, bottle poised over glass.

'Yes please.' Tom turned from his brief inspection of the garden.

David handed round the slim glasses. 'I'll not be a minute, just taking a glass for Pam,' he excused himself and went into the kitchen.

Jenna stole a glance at Tom, not knowing quite what to say for a moment. He had turned back to his study of the garden; to Jenna his back seemed stern and unapproachable.

'Do sit down,' she said at last, sounding abrupt in her own ears. He murmured politely and sat in an armchair, relaxing back into it and crossing his long legs. He watched her silently and she could feel the tell-tale colour rising in her cheeks. There was a magnetic attraction emanating from him; why was he having this effect on her, she was acting like an overgrown schoolgirl! Usually she could hold her own with men.

Suddenly he smiled and the change was magical. Fun peeped out of the depths of those blue eyes, his firm mouth opened to show white teeth which contrasted strongly with his tan.

Jenna's heart did a flip-flop; she was furious with herself for being so gauche, and she hated him for so obviously showing that he knew the effect he was having on her. Though her eyes flashed dangerously she smiled sweetly back at him as she took the opposite chair, moving her legs to the side gracefully. That is, the movement was graceful until she caught her heel in a drooping cretonne hem and lurched forward, spilling her sherry on the grey silk dress.

Tom jumped to his feet, concerned to help her extricate the offending heel. He bent and pulled the torn hem away, holding her ankle to do so.

'Leave me alone!' she hissed, and tugged her foot away from the tingling sensation his hand was producing.

'Goodness!' David had entered the room unnoticed by either of them. 'Are you all right, love?' he continued.

Tom looked up unselfconsciously and got to his feet.

'Jenna caught her foot in the chair cover,' he explained, ignoring the girl's outburst. 'I was freeing it for her.'

David raised his eyebrows and Jenna thought to herself that he could be forgiven for thinking she had been assaulted rather than helped if he had heard her tone with Tom. Wisely however, he said nothing, merely picking up his sherry and taking a sip.

'I'll have to go and change, put this dress in to soak.' Jenna moved to the door. 'Then I'll go and help Pam in the kitchen.' She left the room with as much dignity as she could manage. Upstairs she quickly changed into a simple cotton dress and lower-heeled sandals, then put the grey silk into soak in the bathroom. I'll be lucky if it doesn't stain, she thought gloomily, glancing in the mirror. Her face was flushed, no doubt heightened with the blusher she had applied earlier in the evening. So much for sophistication, she reflected wryly, and washed her face in cold water.

Downstairs she could hear the men talking in the lounge but she went straight into the kitchen. There Pam was hurriedly turning the steaks under the grill. There was the unmistakable smell of charred meat.

'Oh, Jenna, there you are,' said Pam with relief. 'Be a love and mix the salad dressing, will you? These will be ready in a jiffy.' She nodded her head towards the lounge. 'He seems quite nice, doesn't he? And so handsome; these tall, fair men can be devastating can't they?' She rolled her eyes in appreciation, glancing across the table at Jenna who was busy mixing oil and vinegar.

'He's OK.' Jenna's reply was offhand and Pam made a surprised little moue with her lips; normally Jenna was willing to chat about the relative attractions of the doctors David brought home with him.

Just then the smell from the steaks grew stronger and Pam rushed back to the stove. 'Well, these are ready, shall we dish up?' she said.

The meal went off pleasantly enough; the talk was general, about the hospital and the town. Jenna was curious to know why Tom had come to the north-east, his accent had a faint tinge of the West Country. In the end she asked him the direct question.

'What made you decide on Darnton, Mr Yorke?'

Tom paused before answering; they had been discussing the hospital and the question was an abrupt change of subject. Jenna's thoughts had been wandering away from the chat of the dinner-table.

'Well,' he said, after some consideration, 'at first I simply looked for a smallish general hospital; sometimes one gets better experience than in the London teaching hospitals. I've never been north of Reading before and when this position came up I thought I would try for it.' He smiled at his host and hostess. 'And I'm glad I did. The air up here is so good and the countryside so beautiful. I'm sure I'll be happy here.'

A pretty speech, polite too, thought Jenna but her father was obviously delighted. He loved his particular corner of England.

'You must get out and see the dale when you have the chance,' he said now. 'You'll find it well worth it.'

'Perhaps your daughter would be willing to show me the sights.' Tom looked across at Jenna as he spoke, for a moment startling her into feeling at a loss for words. The sudden wail of a child saved her thinking of a reply as Pam rose with a slight grimace.

'There's Annie. I'll just see what's up with her. Do you mind, Jenna—making the coffee?'

Tom looked in some surprise at Jenna;

maybe he expected her to see to Annie, she thought, remembering his mistake of the morning. She did not enlighten him but went out into the kitchen and lit the gas under the percolator. By the time she returned to the dining-room with the tray Pam was already back.

'Annie's OK now, she's gone back to sleep. I don't know what woke her up, she usually sleeps through. I hope she's not sickening for something.'

'Annie's our younger daughter,' explained David. 'Pam and I have been married for three years. Jenna's mother died four years ago.'

Jenna, busy with the coffee-cups, stole an amused glance at Tom, hoping to see him discomfited.

'Coffee, Dr Yorke?' she enquired sweetly. 'Cream and sugar?'

Tom met her eye, but his own betrayed nothing, neither surprise nor discomfort. 'Black, please, Miss Neville. And surely you can call me Tom.'

'Jenna is a third-year student nurse,' explained David. 'At the hospital she even calls me Mr. We can't let them show disrespect, you know!' He grinned mischievously at his daughter, who made to throw a cushion at him.

'A student nurse, eh?' Tom smiled at her. 'And third year. You don't look old enough. When do you take your finals?'

'Not till February. And I'm almost twenty-one.' Jenna sipped her coffee reflectively. 'I'm on casualty at the moment, then I've one more stint on night duty.'

The conversation had reminded her that it was time she began revising in earnest. Jenna had trouble with examinations; at the very thought of her finals butterflies affected her stomach.

'Well, I must get back, thank you for the welcome and the meal.'

Jenna realized that Tom was taking his leave and stood up quickly.

'And you, Nurse Jenna,' he took her hand and kissed it lightly. 'Perhaps I'll see you again soon.' He was flirting outrageously, she thought hotly, and her eyes sparkled with fire. But Pam was grinning in delight at the joke and Jenna contented herself with saying through a bright, set smile, 'Well, of course, Doctor,' while seething underneath. For the life of her she couldn't understand why she should still feel the touch of his lips on her hand, tingling slightly.

When Tom had gone, Jenna began collecting the coffee-cups, rattling them on the tray with temper.

'Steady on!' said Pam in surprise. 'That's the good coffee-set!'

'Oh, sorry, Pam,' Jenna apologized. 'It's just that men like him really make me mad! And that one's so sure he only has to smile and girls will fall over themselves for him!'

'Oh, I don't know,' David commented mildly. 'He seems a good enough sort to me.'

Jenna intercepted the amused glance he

exchanged with Pam

'Well, I'm off to bed,' she said shortly. 'I'm on duty in the morning.' Both her father and Pam only saw the good side of anyone, she thought crossly; it's just as well one member of the family is a little more discerning!

Two

'Hi, Jenna! Did you have a nice day off?'

Jenna's friend Elaine greeted her as she was pinning on her cap in the cloakroom of the accident and emergency unit. Elaine was a newly qualified staff nurse and a friend since they worked together on Jenna's first ward.

'Not bad, thanks, Elaine.' Jenna smiled through the mirror at her friend. 'Many waiting today?'

'A few,' Elaine replied. 'Get the notes from Sally, will you? Dr Stelling will be here any minute.'

'OK, staff.' Satisfied that her cap was secure, Jenna went along the corridor to the casualty reception area. Sally Spinks looked up from her register as Jenna came up to the counter.

'Morning, Jenna,' she said cheerfully. 'How's tricks today then?' Sally was married and in her early forties. She had a thin, athletic figure and pale hair swept up in a bun.

Sally was briskly efficient at her job and now she handed over a batch of casualty forms. 'I've got these for you, dear, nothing wildly urgent.'

'Hello, Sally.' Jenna took the notes and turned to the rows of chairs which held a sprinkling of people waiting with varying degrees of patience.

'Mainly minor,' said Sally behind her, as Jenna checked through the notes to see if anyone merited being seen first. 'The little lad fell off his bike.' She nodded her head towards a harassed-looking woman in her early twenties, obviously about seven months on in pregnancy. She sat with an arm around a boy of about six years old. Snuffily tearful, he held his left arm rigidly against his chest, the classic hold of a fractured humerus, or the upper arm.

'Mam, Mam, it hurts,' he started to wail and leaned against his mother. Jenna moved forward.

'Right then, young man! Jimmy, isn't it? We'll soon have you put to rights.' She smiled at the mother. 'Bring him along to the treatment rooms, Mrs Stephenson. Just follow the red line, it will lead you there.'

'Thanks, nurse.' Mrs Stephenson stood up heavily and took hold of Jimmy's good hand. 'Come on, love, the doctor will soon make you feel better.'

Jimmy forgot to wail and began walking directly along the red line painted on the floor as though it was a tight-rope.

Jenna organized the first half-dozen patients to sit outside the treatment rooms waiting their turn and soon the morning was in full swing. Dr Stelling, the casualty officer, flitted from one room to the next as Elaine and Jenna prepared patients for him.

The nurses were kept busy giving

31

injections, applying bandages to sprained wrists and ankles, and directing patients to X-ray or the plaster-room at Dr Stelling's behest.

'It's just a greenstick fracture, it will be healed in no time,' the doctor reassured Jimmy's mother, after studying the X-ray. 'Give him junior paracetamol tonight if he complains of pain.'

How different he is on duty, thought Jenna, as she applied a sling to Jimmy's arm. Dr Stelling was good at his job, efficient and thorough, but a little impersonal. Off duty he was different.

'A real Don Juan, that one, thinks he's God's gift to the nurses,' Sally had remarked shortly after he arrived to work in the department. 'There'll be trouble, you'll see.'

As usual, Sally was right. Dr Stelling had already left a few broken hearts around the nurses' home.

Her thoughts were interrupted by Sister Bailey, the sister in charge of casualty, who popped her head around the door of the treatment room.

'Go for your break when you've finished there, Jenna. Nurse Foster will relieve you.'

Nurse Foster was an SEN who had worked on casualty for years.

Jenna was pleased to get out into the fresh air; she walked around the building to the canteen instead of going through the hospital, for it was a beautiful morning.

In the canteen she saw Susan sitting alone at a table and took her coffee over.

'Morning, Susan!' Jenna said brightly. 'How are things on the surgical side today?' she said brightly as she took a chair opposite her friend. Susan and Jenna were old friends from school; both were in their third year of training. This morning Susan looked unhappy, she was stirring her coffee moodily, but she looked up and smiled briefly at Jenna

'You don't look too fit.' Jenna spoke bluntly. 'What's up, working too hard?'

'No, it's not that,' sighed Susan. 'It's Charles.'

'Oh Lord, not you too, Susan. I thought you weren't serious about him!'

Jenna was concerned, she knew her friend had been out a couple of times with Charles Stelling but she hadn't realized there was anything more to it than a light-hearted flirtation.

'I wasn't,' Susan said ruefully. 'I didn't think I was getting too involved, it just happened.'

'But what happened? How did he upset you?'

'Oh nothing. Well ... yes, it was something. Oh, I don't know!'

Susan took a gulp of her now cold coffee.

'He asked me out to a party last night, some friend of his. I thought we were really getting on well; you know some people don't understand his manner, but I thought I did. But when we got to the wretched party he spent the whole evening flirting with Staff Simpson; you know, the one on "gynae". I'm sure I could have disappeared altogether and he wouldn't have noticed!'

Jenna looked sympathetically at her friend, but could think of nothing to say that would help.

Men, she thought, as they left the canteen to return to duty! They walked back together as far as the surgical ward where Susan worked.

'Have you met the new surgical registrar yet?' Jenna enquired as they approached the entrance to the ward, more to change the subject than anything else. Her attempt to take Susan's mind off the fickle Dr Stelling seemed to work.

'Oh yes! He did the ward round with your father yesterday. He's really attractive, isn't he? With that blond hair and those deep blue eyes. I love those Nordic-looking men, don't you?'

Jenna laughed as Susan enthused over Tom Yorke. Her heart couldn't be so badly dented if she could talk like this about another man.

'You sound really taken with him anyway!'

'Have you met him yet, Jenna?'

'He was over for dinner yesterday evening,' Jenna nodded. 'I'm not so sure myself; handsome is as handsome does, as they say. He's a bit too sarcastic for my taste, your Dr Yorke.'

Jenna was standing with her back to the corridor leading to the ward and Susan was facing her. Suddenly she noticed that Susan's smile had vanished and she had gone slightly pink as she looked over Jenna's shoulder.

'Is that the truth then, Nurse Neville?'

A deeply masculine voice sounded in Jenna's ear as she swung round to meet the icy gaze of the new registrar, a gaze which contrasted dangerously with his deceptively level tone.

'Perhaps you have something better to do than stand around the corridors discussing the medical staff?' He turned to Susan. 'You have, I know, Nurse Jackson; there is a list for theatre this afternoon, is there not?'

'Yes, doctor.' Susan grinned, not in the least put out, and pushed open the swing doors to the ward and went in.

'Well, Nurse Neville?' The gaze was uncompromising.

'Well, what?' she replied hotly. 'If you will creep up on people and listen in to private conversations, you—' Biting her lip she controlled her temper with some difficulty. The situation left her at a disadvantage, but that had been a bit unfair, the surgical registrar had a right to walk up to the surgical ward!

'Sorry, sir!' she said stiffly. 'I must get back to casualty.' And she fled, leaving him gazing after her sombrely.

'You're off duty on Saturday, aren't you? Saturday evening I mean.' Elaine and Jenna were clearing up in the treatment rooms that afternoon. The flow of casualties had eased and the two girls were taking advantage of the lull to tidy up before going off duty.

'How would you like to go out for a meal, then maybe on to a disco?' Elaine continued.

'Well.' Jenna hesitated, she wasn't too keen on discos really, but it would make a change.

'Oh, go on,' urged Elaine. 'You haven't got a date, have you?' Elaine had recently broken off with her boyfriend and was finding this left gaps in her social life.

'OK,' Jenna decided. 'I'll ask Susan if she wants to come, if that's all right. She could do with a bit of cheering up.'

'Great! That's a date then.' Elaine glanced around the room. 'All shipshape. We'll just report to Sister, then I'm off.'

It was a beautiful evening as Jenna left the hospital and she decided to walk instead of taking the bus. Though she was tired after the long day on her feet, the fresh cool air was invigorating and she strolled along thinking about nothing in particular, simply enjoying the walk.

Jenna was about a mile from home when the red MG pulled up beside her and Tom Yorke leaned over and opened the passenger door.

'Jump in, I'll give you a lift home,' he said pleasantly.

Jenna began to refuse then realized it sounded churlish after their last encounter, so murmuring a rather ungracious thanks she got in beside him.

She was conscious of the magnetic attraction this man held for her, her skin tingled as she brushed against his shoulder in the small car. Quickly she huddled against the door, trying to keep a space between them.

Tom glanced down at her with raised eyebrows, then returned his attention to the road without comment.

'Surely I must be taking you out of your way,' she said stiffly, to break the lengthening silence.

'Not far out of my way,' he replied as he pulled up before the gate to the Nevilles' house. 'Besides, I wanted to ask you something.' He climbed out of the car and opened her door for her. 'It's my weekend off and I hoped you would be kind enough to show a stranger around the dale. With perhaps dinner on Saturday evening?'

He smiled down at Jenna as she got out of the car, those deep blue eyes alight with charm. Easy charm, thought Jenna suddenly as she remembered their encounter at the hospital!

She turned away and began taking an inordinate interest in the 'Gloire de Dijon' rose climbing over the garden wall, the sweet scent of the rose combined with the smell of newly-cut grass from the lawn creating a headiness on the still evening air.

'I have made other arrangements for Saturday evening, and I'm working during the day.' She lifted her chin and faced him.

'Oh, I see. A boyfriend, is it?' His tone was smooth and expressionless. Jenna refrained from telling him to mind his own business.

'A friend. Well, thanks for the lift, Dr Yorke.' She turned to walk up the drive.

'Hang on a minute! I take it you are free on Sunday?'

He was being surprisingly persistent and fleetingly she wondered why.

'You do have this Sunday free?'

Jenna paused for an undecided moment; had he been checking up on her off-duty? 'Well, I ...'

'We can have lunch in the country and then spend the day touring the local beauty spots.' His tone was persuasive.

'Hello there, you two!' Pam appeared around the corner of the house, a pair of secateurs in her hand. 'Brought Jenna home, have you, Tom? Do come in for a drink, I could do with an excuse to leave

41

the rest of the roses until tomorrow.'

'Sorry, not this evening if you don't mind, Mrs Neville. I have rather a lot of work to catch up on.' Tom turned back to the car. 'I take it that that is arranged then, Jenna I'll pick you up about ten o'clock.'

Jenna's eyes registered surprise but before she could demur he was in his car and away, leaving her gazing after him.

'What was that about?' Pam asked curiously, then catching sight of Jenna's expression added hastily, 'Sorry! I didn't mean to pry! Don't tell me if you don't want to.' She tucked her arm into Jenna's. 'Come on, we'll have a nice long drink anyway.'

'It's all right, Pam. He just asked me out on Sunday. The Lord knows why. Maybe he just wants to keep in with the boss's daughter.'

'Get along with you! You are under-estimating your charms!' scoffed Pam, but as Jenna followed her into the house she couldn't help feeling that there was some truth in the remark.

The following Saturday morning the accident and emergency department began quietly enough, there were only a few minor injuries to deal with before lunch. Jenna and Elaine found themselves again on the same duty and the morning dragged on slowly. It was so quiet that Sister sent them off to lunch together.

'If anything comes up I'll be able to manage,' Sister said. 'There's a football match this afternoon, Darnton are at home. You never know, we may all be needed if there is any bother.'

The two nurses collected their cloaks and made their way over for lunch.

'Where do you fancy eating tonight, Jenna?' Elaine asked as she took a helping of shepherd's pie onto her tray. 'I can't afford to eat at the Manor though!' She smiled ruefully. 'I'll be glad when it's the end of the month and I'm in funds again.' The Manor was a large hotel on the edge of town with plush restaurants and a disco in the basement.

'Let's go Chinese then,' suggested Jenna. 'Susan likes Chinese.' Jenna had persuaded Susan to forget about Charles Stelling for one night and have the evening out with them.

'OK. Then we can go on to the disco at the Manor,' agreed Elaine. 'We can go in my car. I'll pick you up, and Susan too of course. Can you let her know?'

Elaine's car had been a present from her parents when she passed her finals. It was her pride and joy, but also one of the reasons she was always short of money.

'She's off today. I'll ring her at home. Eight o'clock shall I say?'

'Yes, that gives us time to eat before we go to the Manor disco. It won't get going until about eleven.'

Fortunately Sister's fears of trouble at the football match proved groundless and the department continued quiet during the rest of the day. Consequently Jenna felt quite fresh and was looking forward to a good Saturday night out with her friends.

By eight o'clock Jenna was ready and waiting for Elaine, freshly bathed and with her hair piled on top of her head and held with a diamanté butterfly clip. The stain had come out of the grey silk outfit and it had cleaned up well. Now she smoothed it down over her hips as she checked it in the hall mirror.

The tooting of a car horn heralded the arrival of Elaine and Susan; calling her goodbyes to Pam and her father she slipped out of the house.

They ate Chinese at a restaurant in the marketplace, agreeing to a meal for three at a set price to save money. Susan was bright and cheerful, she seemed determined to forget about her troubles and have a good time. So the atmosphere was light-hearted and they were laughing and joking as they left the restaurant and drove the short distance to the Manor. Susan was deep into the continuing story of Maggie, an old lady of some character who had been brought into Casualty the previous Saturday evening.

'You remember her, surely, Jenna; happy as a queen and singing at the top of her voice, despite a fractured tib. and fib?'

Jenna remembered her only too well and now she nodded with a smile. She had had the job of emptying Maggie's stomach before she went to theatre to have her leg set; it was difficult to forget someone when you had aspirated what looked like pure brown ale, four pints of it, from someone's stomach, while that person was grinning cheerfully all the while, seeming oblivious to the pain from a compound fracture of the lower leg.

'I had a terrible job trying to hold her leg still, it was quite weird, and all the time Charlie Stelling looking on with that disdainful expression on his face as though he could hardly bear to touch her—'

Jenna stopped abruptly, seeing the changed expression on Susan's face. How could she have been so careless as to mention Dr Stelling just when Susan seemed to have put him out of her mind?

But Susan paused only for a moment, then the smile returned to her face. 'Yes, well, she wasn't feeling so good when she woke up the next day, I can tell you! No, though today she was sitting up in bed leading the others in a rousing chorus of "Cushy Butterfield", but believe me I wouldn't like to repeat her version of the words!

'Sister marched down the ward wearing her frostiest look, but that old reprobate wasn't the least put out. She paused only long enough to ask if Sister had any stout in the fridge! "By ..." she said, "what I wouldn't give for a nice glass of stout!"

'You should have seen Sister's face!' laughed Susan, and they all three giggled merrily at the thought; Sister on Susan's ward was definitely of the old school, stern and disapproving.

They had reached the Manor by this time, and as they got out of the car a group of boys climbed out of a battered old Mini at the other end of the car-park. They all reached the entrance to the Manor together, and Jenna saw they were old school-friends.

'Hi, Susan! Jenna!' The boy grinning lazily at them from under a spiky mop of dark hair politely opened the door for them, and Jenna realized it was Wayne Johns. They had gone out together a few times when they were in the fifth form at school; Wayne had been the heart-throb of the school at the time and Jenna had been quite flattered to receive his attentions. But she hadn't seen him for years, and now as she looked up at him she was dismayed to see that his good-looks were already a little blotchy, and his eyes were not so clear as she remembered.

'Hello, Wayne, how are you doing now?' she asked as Susan added her greeting and they all swept into the entrance of the hotel together and made for the staircase which led down to the disco. They chattered and laughed together as they went; it was fun to meet Wayne and his friends again, bringing back memories of school and good times they had had together. Jenna just giggled mischievously as Elaine caught her eye and rolled her own expressively. Obviously Elaine was not too keen on the company.

'Oh Lord, look who's here.' Susan spoke in a low tone and nodded towards the door of the dining-room. Just emerging were Dr Yorke and a companion, a beautiful woman in a white dress which showed off to perfection her golden tan and long golden hair which hung in a shining coil over one shoulder.

Jenna had been laughing at a remark of Wayne's as she turned to see who it was, and now she found herself meeting Dr Yorke's rather sardonic gaze. His lips twisted slightly as he acknowledged the nurses, while his companion murmured something to him with an amused expression on her beautiful face.

'Come on, Jenna what are you waiting for?' Wayne was already halfway down the staircase and now he paused and looked back at her enquiringly.

'Coming,' said Jenna and stole one more glance behind her, but the doctor and his friend had disappeared into the lounge.

'Whew!' said Susan. 'I wonder who that was with Dr Yorke? Quite something, wasn't she?'

'I didn't notice!'

Jenna spoke shortly and Susan looked at her in surprise, but wisely decided to say nothing. The three girls went on into the disco where Elaine deliberately led them to a table away from Wayne and his friends. They were not so easily deterred though, and hung around most of the time.

Nevertheless the girls enjoyed the music and dancing; even Elaine began to smile a little at Wayne's jokes and Jenna was pleased to see that Susan seemed to have forgotten about Dr Stelling and was throwing herself into the spirit of the evening.

'Maybe it's time we were thinking about leaving,' suggested Elaine. They were back at their table having a break from dancing and Wayne and his friends had disappeared for the moment.

'Well, I am feeling a bit tired now,' admitted Susan, who a minute before had been putting her all into dancing. 'It would be a good idea to slip away now.'

It *was* a good time to leave, thought Jenna, as she nodded and picked up her bag ready to go. Wayne's jokes had been getting wilder as the evening progressed and his speech became more blurred.

As they came out into the cool air Susan drew a sigh of relief.

'That's good!' she said. 'Wasn't it hot in there? Still, I think we all had a good time; at least, I know I did.'

'Mmh.' Jenna nodded in agreement.

'Well, I could have done without Wayne

Johns and co. Did you see how much they were drinking? I'm surprised they are still on their feet!'

'They were drinking a lot,' said Jenna 'It's a pity really, at school we all thought he was the one who would get on and be something special, he's clever and good-looking; but now he seems on the road to nowhere.'

'Well,' said Susan, thankfully relaxing into the back seat of the Fiesta. 'People change as they grow up.' She yawned widely. 'Now all I can think of is bed; thank the Lord I'm off tomorrow! You are too, aren't you, Jenna?'

'That's right.'

'Got anything planned?' asked Susan. 'If not, perhaps we can meet up. Or have you got a date?'

'Well ...' Jenna was reminded of Tom Yorke and his high-handed way of making a date.

'Oh, it's all right,' said Susan quickly. 'It's high time I visited my family anyway.'

Jenna let it go at that; she wasn't sure whether she should ring Tom up and tell him she was not going, but in the end she had to admit that there was something in her which wanted to go, was fascinated by the idea of a whole day in his company.

Three

Jenna woke next morning to a beautiful day with the sun streaming through the window. She showered and dressed in a full-skirted, white cotton dress which had a narrow blue belt and blue and white sandals to match, arriving down to breakfast with her dark hair loose and brushed until it shone.

'My, you are looking pretty this morning,' commented Pam, who was deftly spooning scrambled eggs into Annie's open mouth.

'Me do it!' Annie made a grab for the spoon, sending particles of egg flying over the table.

'Righto, darling, you do it,' said Pam resignedly. 'No mess now.' She took a dish-cloth from the sink and cleaned up the spilt egg, then looked sideways at Jenna. 'All this in aid of Tom Yorke?' she remarked slyly.

Jenna looked slightly annoyed as she slipped a couple of slices of bread into the toaster. 'Rubbish!' she said firmly. 'This dress is nothing special, I've had it for ages!' Which was really true, though she had been keeping it for a special occasion. Pam smiled in a maddening sort of way and Jenna decided to ignore her. Walking over to Annie she dropped a kiss on top of the blonde curly head.

'Hello, my pet!' she said, and Annie grinned engagingly through the ring of scrambled egg and butter which was smeared on her face.

'Your father's down at the hospital,' Pam volunteered. 'There was a road traffic accident last night and he was called in. A young boy, I understand.'

Jenna looked up from spreading toast with butter and marmalade. 'A bad accident?'

'I think there was just the one casualty. You know David doesn't discuss his work much with me, but evidently he had internal injuries. Anyway, he's gone to check on him.'

'Poor Dad! Another Sunday morning gone. Still, I suppose with his registrar off for the weekend ...'

'Speaking of which, you had better get a move on, my girl, it's almost ten o'clock; isn't that when Tom said he would call for you?'

'That's right. Though if he has to wait it will be his own fault, he didn't consult me about the time! It might be a bit chilly on the top of the moor.'

Jenna was looking through her wardrobe, finally deciding on a light-blue anorak as the weather could be changeable this late in the summer, when Pam called up the stairs.

'Jenna! Tom is here!'

Stupidly, Jenna felt her heart do a little flip and frowned at herself in the mirror. Don't let him get at you, she warned herself; remember he's not really interested in you, except as your father's daughter. Besides, consider the vision he was with last night! She fixed a nonchalant smile on her face and then, satisfied with her reflection, went down the stairs to meet him.

Tom was leaning against the kitchen doorframe with his back to the hall; he was chatting quietly with Pam who was busy cleaning up Annie. He looked long-legged and athletic, dressed casually in jeans and a short-sleeved shirt which showed his bronzed forearms. He didn't turn immediately as Jenna came up behind him.

'Good-morning, Dr Yorke.' She spoke coolly. 'I'm ready when you are.'

He straightened and turned to her lazily, a half-smile playing round his mouth. 'Good-morning to you, Nurse Neville. Certainly I'm ready.'

'Don't you two think you should be

on first-name terms, at least when you are out together?' Pam laughed. 'I don't think hospital discipline will be damaged by that.'

'It is a little ridiculous,' agreed Tom. 'Well, shall we go, Jenna?'

The pair made their goodbyes to Pam and Annie and soon they were in Tom's car and heading out of the town and onto the road climbing gently up into Weardale.

At first little was said except for Jenna giving directions but when they reached the open road leading up into Wolsingham she sat back and enjoyed the feel of the wind in her hair and the sunshine on her face. The top was wound back on the car and though it was slightly chilly it was delightful.

'Did you have a good time with your friends last night?' Tom spoke smoothly without taking his eyes from the road, and she stole a quick glance at his face.

'Yes, thank you.'

'You certainly seemed to be when I

saw you at the Manor. Though I'm not sure if your father would approve of your friends.'

Jenna's temper rose. 'What do you mean, I was with Susan and Elaine. And it's none of your business!' She stared out of the window at the rolling hills and the River Wear running alongside the road. But her thoughts were boiling and she couldn't keep her tongue still.

'I noticed it didn't take you long to find a replacement for dinner either!'

He turned angry eyes on her before slowing to negotiate the bridge which took them into Wolsingham. Then suddenly he chuckled, his mood seeming to change altogether.

'All right, all right!' He spoke quietly now, his tone more amused than angry. 'Let's call a truce, shall we? It's a glorious day and there won't be so many left this year. What do you say?' He pulled over onto the cobbles of the main street of the old dales town and stopped the car, though keeping the engine running. Pulling on the handbrake he turned to her and put his hand over hers, and once again she found herself drowning in his deep blue gaze.

'Pax?'

Jenna's anger melted away, her hand tingled to his touch. She couldn't help herself, she had to agree with him.

'Pax!' she said.

Tom squeezed her hand and returned to his driving.

'Good girl,' he said. 'Now, where do I go from here?'

'We can carry on up the dale through Frosterley and Stanhope in Weardale to the high moor,' suggested Jenna. 'It depends how far you want to go really. Over the top into Cumbria and down to Alston, or across the fell and back down Teesdale, whichever you like.'

'Well, we'll just drive and see where we end up then, shall we? So long as there is somewhere we can eat lunch.'

'We can always get a pub lunch in

St Johns Chapel or in Alston,' Jenna volunteered.

They climbed higher on the gently rising road to Frosterley, the sun warm on their heads and shoulders; Jenna began to relax, letting the breeze lift her hair, it was a heavenly day. Tom drove slowly, looking about him with interest; luckily there was very little traffic on the road and so he could take a leisurely attitude to the drive, slowing down at times to gaze at the view.

The ground rose steeply at the side of the road, with rocky outcrops and perpendicular cliffs high above them on the right, while the river bubbled along beside them on the left.

'Frosterley was famous for the black marble which was quarried here, and of course those rounded mounds are man-made too, from the days when lead-mining was the main industry in the dale.' She broke off abruptly. Oh Lord, she thought, I'm beginning to sound like a travelogue.

But Tom seemed genuinely interested. 'Yet they look so pretty, covered in grass, you would hardly believe they were spoil-heaps once.'

They drove on through the village and on into Stanhope in Weardale. Further on, at St Johns Chapel, they stopped and walked around in the warm sunshine before having lunch in the King's Head, a traditional roast-beef lunch with fluffy Yorkshire puddings and oodles of gravy.

Jenna was feeling more relaxed in his company, Tom was charming and attentive. She found herself telling him little anecdotes about Annie, her baby sister, who had some funny, entertaining ways, as do most toddlers; and he listened, smiling gently into her animated face with those oh so disturbing dark-blue eyes.

'And you, what about your family, Tom?' Jenna took a sip of her coffee and sat back in her chair.

'Oh, I'm a Devon man myself. My parents still live in Torquay. I've one sister, who's married to a doctor.'

'You'll be well used to moors then, coming from Devon.'

'Yes, but it is very different up here. Wilder somehow.' He replaced his coffee-cup on his saucer and beckoned to the waiter for the bill. 'Let's get on then, shall we? It's pity to waste too much of this lovely day.'

'This lovely day,' Jenna echoed silently as they drove up to the top of the high moor and stopped the car on a patch of turf by the side of the narrow road lined with snow-poles. The moor stretched endlessly to the horizon on either side, purple with the heather, patched with clumps of brown bracken.

They walked along old tracks as sheep bleated and bounded out of their way, the air exhilarating and the turf springy to their steps. They found an old abandoned farmhouse and fantasized about the family which had lived there so many years before. There was a rowan tree planted at the gateway of the old farm, standing sturdy on that otherwise treeless fell.

'To ward off evil spirits,' said Jenna. 'To bring good luck.' But did it bring good luck, she wondered? The family had had to move away, and the land would be incorporated in a large sheep-farm now. As if to echo her thought, a sheep wandered out of the kitchen doorway and Jenna shivered involuntarily.

'Cold?' said Tom instantly. 'It is quite bracing up here. Do you want to go back to the car?'

'It's nothing,' said Jenna 'No, let's wander a little further.'

They came to a sudden dip in the moor, hidden until they were almost upon it; a little burn twinkled its way down over stones, into a tiny wooded valley.

'Let's sit a while, it's so peaceful here,' said Tom, and they sat on the sun-warmed flat rock, sheltered from the breeze.

'A fairy place,' murmured Tom, and took hold of her hand and held it to his cheek. Jenna shivered in a strange anticipation; she felt under some enchantment; the little valley; the cry of a curlew overhead; and above all, the touch of his hand on hers. Speechless, she gazed up into his eyes.

'Baa ...' A sheep, bounding down the steep slope of the ghyll, almost on top of them, baa-ing in startled surprise which almost matched her own, brought Jenna to her feet, the moment shattered. She laughed shakily as the sheep decided they were no threat to her and proceeded to graze the lush grass by the stream.

'Jenna?'

Tom came to his feet also, reaching out a hand to her, his expression questioning. But Jenna ignored it and began to climb back up the bank side, her feelings chaotic; she had to sort herself out.

'Come on,' she said. 'I'll race you to the car!'

He watched her for a moment, his expression unreadable, then took the slope with long bounding strides, easily overtaking her, so that when she arrived breathless and laughing he was there holding open the door for her in mock gallantry.

Jenna was quiet as they drove back into Durham County by Teesdale as the afternoon shadows lengthened.

At High Force they climbed up the side of the waterfall, watching the peaty water roar into white foam as it went into the falls. The sun was setting and dusk settled around them.

'Here, take my hand,' said Tom, as they descended to the path once again, and the sudden touch of him made her stumble slightly against him. Tom groaned and gathered her into his arms, there, halfway up the steps, as the water roared and the darkness fell. Jenna felt herself melting into him as she lifted her face to his kiss and his mouth came down on hers, softly, questioning at first, then hard and demanding as his passion flared. She was held against the rippling firmness of his athletic body as her arms moved almost of their own volition to slide around his neck and into his crisp hair. She was carried along on a tide of feeling which she was incapable of resisting.

It was Tom who released her mouth and relaxed his hold on her, holding her slightly away from him and gazing down into her eyes as through trying to read her mind.

'Jenna?' he said, as he had that afternoon, his tone low and vibrant. She didn't reply, it was taking all her efforts to regain control of her emotions, to bring down her racing heartbeats. What on earth was the matter with her? Instinctively, she drew back into herself, and laughed lightly, remembering his dinner companion of the evening before, his sarcasm. He was not really interested in her.

Immediately Tom dropped his hands. 'We'll go then,' he said, his voice without expression. They walked back up the path to the car and she waited silently while he raised the hood. It was full night now and the air was cool.

They drove back swiftly along the quiet road; Tom seemed like a stranger to her as he sat unspeaking, his eyes on the road. The magic of the afternoon had evaporated, she thought miserably, and cast about in her mind for something to say, anything to break the ice.

'They are really quite different, the two dales,' she said at last.

'Yes?'

'Oh yes, they are,' she gabbled on. 'The streams in Weardale are burns, but they are becks in Teesdale, like Yorkshire. And you saw how Teesdale is softer somehow, not so wild.' This elicited no response, so she chattered on.

'The "hope" in Stanhope and Ireshopeburn, all the names with "hope" in them, well, it means upland valley; it's pronounced "up", not "hope" as in faith, hope and charity.'

'Is that a fact!'

Was that mirth in his voice? He was laughing at her. She glared at his profile outlined against the moonlight, but she could see nothing in his face, perhaps she was mistaken. She subsided into silence once again.

'Shall we stop for dinner in Barnard Castle?' Tom asked as the lights of the town appeared in the distance. 'Or are you too tired? In a hurry to get home?'

He doesn't want to be bothered, she thought miserably, he just wants to get back himself. Well, she wasn't going to let him know she didn't want the day to come to an end.

'I'd rather go straight home if you don't mind,' she said stiffly. 'I have a slight headache.'

They were going through the brightly-lit streets of the town by this time and he slowed the car and turned to look at her critically.

'If that's what you want,' he said. 'Sure now?'

'Yes. I want to get home.'

Tom shrugged and turned his attention to the car. He picked up speed as they approached open countryside, and it seemed no time at all before he pulled up at Jenna's home.

'Thank you for a lovely day,' she said formally, like a little girl. 'You don't mind if I don't ask you in?' She held out her hand to him.

'Not at all.' He took it in his firm, surgeon's hand and squeezed it gently. 'We'll do it again sometime.'

'Well, I am going to be rather busy,' said Jenna 'I must start working for my finals, do some revision.'

Tom raised his eyebrows. 'I thought you said they were in February?'

'I know five months seems a long time, but I'm not very good with examinations, so I want to have it all off pat.'

'But ... Yes, of course.' He nodded formally. 'Well, no doubt I'll see you around the hospital.' He turned on his heel and got back into the car, driving off immediately.

Jenna watched his tail-lights disappearing along the road, her feelings mixed. She knew she had offended him; he was sceptical of her plea of too much work. If he had been genuinely interested in her she had spoilt it for herself. She walked up the drive despondently, more so because of the contrast with the lovely day's outing.

'That you, Jenna?' Pam called from the sitting-room as she let herself in through the front door. 'Have you had anything to eat?'

'Hello.' Jenna walked into the room and flopped down on the settee beside her father, who was sitting comfortably in his carpet slippers reading the Sunday papers. He had been at the hospital earlier in the day and this was the first opportunity he had had to relax and read them.

'I haven't eaten actually, but don't worry, I'll get myself a sandwich in a minute,' Jenna said to Pam who was also relaxing in an easy-chair, watching the television.

'There's a salad in the fridge, and some cold chicken.' Pam glanced at Jenna 'You all right, love? You look a bit pale.'

'Just a bit tired, it's nothing. Hungry, I should think.'

'Did you enjoy your day?'

'Oh yes, it was lovely on the moors. And we had a good lunch in St John's Chapel.'

'I thought you might bring Tom in.' Her father looked up from his paper. 'I wouldn't have minded a chat with him.'

'I was tired,' Jenna said quickly, standing up and picking up her sweater from the back of the settee where she had draped it. 'He did offer to give me dinner in Barnard Castle, but I think he really wanted to get home.' She dropped a kiss on top of his head. 'I think I'll just put something on a tray and take it up to my room if you don't mind. Goodnight, both!'

He shot a surprised look at her retreating back, then turned to Pam and shrugged.

'Perhaps they didn't get along too well after all,' she said in low tones. 'Funny, I thought they were interested in each other.'

'Come on!' David grinned. 'For goodness' sake, they hardly know each other yet; it's a bit early for matchmaking!'

Pam grinned and went back to her television viewing. Never mind, she thought to herself, she was sure there had been a spark of something between Tom and Jenna when she had watched them together that morning.

Jenna collected a plate of chicken and salad and carried it up to her room. She picked at it half-heartedly as her mind went over the day, the depth of feeling which had taken hold of her when Tom had kissed her. Was that love? She picked up a piece of chicken on her fork and looked at it before putting it down again. She really couldn't face it. She was tired; being out in the fresh air and tramping over the moors, that was all it was; though she could not deny the tremendous physical attraction Tom had for her.

'Jenna?' Pam interrupted her thoughts as she knocked on the bedroom door. 'I thought I would come up for the tray.' She noticed the almost untouched meal. 'But you haven't eaten anything! Do you want a couple of aspirin? Is your headache bad? I could ask your father to have a look at you.'

'No, no; don't fuss, Pam.' Jenna spoke a little too sharply. 'Sorry, I didn't mean to snap. I think I'll just have an early night. It's nothing, really; we had a huge lunch, that's all. A good night's sleep and I'll be as good as new.'

'Well, if you're sure ...' Pam picked up the tray. 'Maybe you're right.'

'Yes. Thanks, Pam. Goodnight then.'

'Goodnight, Jenna.'

As the door closed behind Pam, Jenna undressed for bed with a sense somehow of anticlimax. It had been such a lovely day. The memory of it was a kaleidoscope of impressions: the little, wooded valley; the old abandoned farmhouse; the wide expanse of the high moor. And over all, the memory of the episode on the steps by the waterfall, the sound of the water roaring down to the pool below, the feel of Tom's arms around her, his mouth on hers. As she climbed into bed, sure she wouldn't sleep, the memory stayed with her; when she closed her eyes his face floated on her eyelids, she felt languorous, her breasts ached.

Whether through a surfeit of emotion or fresh moorland air, Jenna did fall asleep almost instantly; when her father came up half an hour later and listened at her bedroom door, all he could hear was the deep, regular breathing of sleep.

Four

'Did you have a nice day off?' enquired Elaine as they prepared the treatment rooms for casualties on Monday morning. 'You'd just have a nice lazy day, I expect, after Saturday night.'

'I went out as a matter of fact,' said Jenna, though she felt slightly reluctant about telling Elaine even though they were friends.

'Yes?' Elaine looked up from her dressing-packs in some surprise. 'You didn't say you had anything arranged. Where did you go?'

'We had a day out in the dales. It was a super day, wasn't it?'

'It was, lovely. But who's we?' Elaine persisted.

'Dr Yorke asked me to show him the

local beauty spots,' Jenna admitted.

'Dr Yorke! I say!' Elaine's eyes opened wide. 'You are a dark horse! You never said a word about that!'

'There was nothing to tell! He wanted someone to show him around and I was there; he knew me because of my father.'

'Oh yes, of course. I suppose that's one advantage of being the daughter of a consultant surgeon, you will get the chance of meeting all the dishy young surgeons on your own home ground. And they don't come any dishier than Dr Yorke!'

Jenna got no chance to answer as Sister came in just then with the first-year student nurse newly assigned to the department.

'Show her where things are and generally look out for her this morning, will you, Jenna?' she said. 'You'll soon get into the way of it,' she added kindly to the nervous young girl. 'Nurse Neville will keep you right.' It often fell to Jenna's lot to see to newcomers, she was naturally sympathetic and remembered her own first days only too well.

'Better you than me,' murmured Elaine, as she was going over to Sally's reception desk to bring round the first few casualties. 'We'll hear all about yesterday at coffee-time then?' She grinned over her shoulder as she went and Jenna frowned ferociously before turning to her new protégé.

'Come along then and I'll give you a brief run down on the place, then we will be working with Dr Stelling this morning.'

They were soon immersed in the usual flow of minor injuries, the first-year nurse, Jane, applying dressings and helping with injections on Dr Stelling's instructions and under Jenna's watchful eye. Jenna was patient with her and she began to gain confidence in what she was doing. She was quite pretty, Jenna realized, with fair, pale looks; when she lost her nervousness she was attractive.

Obviously Charlie Stelling thought so

too, for during a lull he began chatting her up, bringing a slight blush to her cheeks. Jenna was annoyed, the man seemed as though he could not pass up any opportunity to make a conquest.

'If you don't mind, Dr Stelling,' she said frostily, 'I will show nurse around the department, and the plaster room.'

Jane looked slightly surprised, they had already been round once, but she followed Jenna out without demur.

'You want to watch out for Charlie Stelling,' Jenna said grimly. 'He thinks he's Don Juan. Charming he may be, but be warned.'

'I can look after myself,' Jane asserted.

'Yes, well it was only a friendly warning.' Jenna said no more as they made their way past the crowded orthopaedic clinic. Glancing over the patients she noticed Jimmy Stephenson and his mother sitting patiently in the front row. Jimmy's mother looked more harassed than ever as she shifted uncomfortably on her seat, and

Jimmy wriggled about on his.

'Hang on a minute,' said Jenna, 'I'll just have a word with Jimmy. He fractured his humerus last week, he must be here for a check-up.'

'Hello, Mrs Stephenson, how are you getting on?' said Jenna as she sat down in the next chair.

'Oh, hello, nurse. I'm all right really, it's just uncomfortable sitting for long when I'm this far on. I wish to heaven it was all over.' She sighed heavily.

'I shouldn't think you'll be long now,' said Jenna, trying to encourage her. 'Jimmy in for a check-up?'

'Will they take the bandage off, nurse?' piped up Jimmy. 'I'm fed up with it, I am.'

'Well, it depends on the doctor, Jimmy,' said Jenna. It was only a greenstick fracture, she remembered, it was probably healing nicely.

'Jimmy Stephenson,' called the orthopaedic nurse.

'There you are then.' Jenna smiled at Jimmy. 'Good luck now.' And they followed the nurse into the consulting-room.

'Can't you leave her alone?' Jenna had sent Jane off to the pathology lab. on a message and for the moment she was alone in the treatment room with Charlie Stelling.

'What do you mean, nurse, I haven't done anything yet!'

'Why do you have to make a play for every new nurse who is at all passable?' Jenna was annoyed, and she thought fleetingly about Susan; why couldn't she see through this shallow man?

'I don't think it's any of your business!' snapped Dr Stelling, as he sat back from writing up a patient's notes. 'Or are you jealous, Nurse Neville?'

'Nothing of the sort! I just don't like to see them taken in.'

'Mmh, yes. I understand it's the surgical staff which interests you more at the moment!' He smirked at her knowingly. 'Why shouldn't I enjoy myself anyway? You know as well as I do that the only reason most of these nurses are here is to catch themselves a doctor for a husband! But Charles Stelling is going to prove a difficult fish to hook!'

Jenna glared at him, speechless. It was no good, she was never going to get through to him. He simply smiled back at her, malice lurking at the back of his eyes.

'I'm going along to check on Jane,' she said at last; she really felt that if she stayed there another minute she would slap his face, and what an uproar that would cause, she thought grimly; student nurse attacks casualty officer! Sister would be pleased!

But Jane was already outside the door. 'Sister says we should go for coffee now,' she announced. 'Staff will wait until we get back.'

'Well, thank heaven for that,' said Jenna. Jane turned startled eyes on her.

'What do you mean? Is something wrong?'

'No, no.' Jenna managed a low laugh. 'I just mean I'm dying for a cup of coffee.' But what she had really meant was that at least she was spared Elaine's questions about Tom for a while. She was fed up with the medical profession altogether, at least the younger members of it. Did the other doctors feel like that about the nurses? In particular, did Tom? She shook her head as though to clear it of such ideas. Jane was studying her face curiously, and with an effort Jenna smiled. 'Come on, let's get that coffee.'

As they came back into the department by reception, Sally called them over.

'It's been a sudden rush this last few minutes; a man rushed straight from work with an acute abdomen; a scalded hand; and assorted minor injuries.' She grinned cheerfully. 'Just so that you don't get a shock when you get round to the treatment rooms.'

Jenna groaned. 'Oh well, better get on. Come on, Jane.'

Elaine was applying Flamazine to the hand of a white-faced, middle-aged woman. Jenna shot a quick glance at it as she went into the treatment room. Only second-degree burns, she noticed.

'I don't know how I could have done such a stupid thing, nurse,' the woman was saying. 'I was just putting the coffee-pot back on the ring when it tipped and the hot coffee went all over my hand. I've never been so careless before, it must not have been balanced properly.'

Elaine worked on deftly. 'Well, you are lucky it's no worse; you'll watch it another time.' She looked up at Jenna. 'I'm glad to see you back. Dr Stelling is next door examining the acute abdomen. See if he needs you, will you? Jane stay with me for a while, I may need you.'

In the next room Dr Stelling was bending

over a white-faced man on a stretcher. He was using his stethoscope and sounding out the man's abdomen, so Jenna moved quietly to the opposite side of the stretcher and waited. Normally, acute surgical or medical cases were admitted straight into the wards, but occasionally there was a case such as this one where the patient was at work or collapsed in the street and was sent directly into hospital.

Jenna looked at the patient for any signs or symptoms. He was obviously in pain, his face showed that all too clearly, and his fists clenched and unclenched as the doctor listened and probed. At last Dr Stelling was satisfied; he straightened up and took the stethoscope out of his ears.

'Oh it's you, Nurse Neville,' he said, his tone impersonal, as though their previous argument had never been. 'I'm going to ring for Dr Yorke. Strangulated hernia, I think. Stay with him while I phone?'

He nodded at the man on the stretcher, and sauntered out of the room. The man turned anxious eyes on Jenna.

'What did he say it was, nurse?'

'It's not really serious,' she hastened to assure him. 'He thinks it may be a rupture. But don't worry, we'll take care of you now.'

He looked at her rather dubiously. 'Does it mean an operation?'

'We don't know yet. But Dr Yorke will soon be here and he will tell you all about it. Please don't worry.'

Charlie Stelling treats the patients like cattle, not human beings, she thought rebelliously. Well, maybe that was going a bit far, but really, why couldn't he have reassured the man himself?

Fortunately, Tom was down to see the patient within ten minutes, when the difference in his approach to that of Dr Stelling was marked. He immediately put the man at his ease, explaining what he was doing and why.

'I'm afraid your rupture has twisted, cutting off the passage through the gut.

That is what is causing all the trouble. But don't worry, we will have you right as rain, though it means an operation straight away. Nothing to worry about though.'

The worry faded from the man's eyes; now he knew what was the matter it was just a case of getting it over with. He managed a smile at Tom.

'Thank you, doctor.'

'Well, we'll soon have you on the ward and prepared for theatre. You'll soon be out of pain.'

He nodded to Jenna, who handed him the notes. 'Surgical 4. I have notified them. See you later then,' he said to the patient, and went out to the office phone to check with Mr Neville.

Jenna went to call a porter to take the stretcher to the ward. Coming back to the treatment rooms she was surprised to see Wayne Johns lounging on one of the chairs by the door.

'Hi there, Jenna,' he said cheerfully, without standing up. 'Susan said you were working on Casualty so I thought I'd nip along to see you.'

'What on earth are you doing here?' Jenna was not too pleased. 'Is there something wrong?'

'Come and sit down for a minute, surely you can spare a minute,' said Wayne.

'Of course I can't, I'm on duty!'

Wayne stood up and leaned against the corridor wall. 'Oh come on, Jenna I came to see Mike; you know, he was with us on Saturday night. He got a bit too much to drink and had an argument with a car. Anyway, he can go home today. And that reminds me, where were you when it happened? You disappeared a bit sharpish, you and your friends; you might have been able to help.'

'It happened on Saturday night?' said Jenna, that must have been the RTA her father was called out to, she thought.

'Yes, as we came out of the disco. But he is OK now. I thought we could maybe have a night out, me and you, just like the old days, eh, Jenna?' He grinned lazily, very sure of himself.

'I don't think so, Wayne, really,' said Jenna 'Now will you please go? I have work to do.'

'I'll go when you say yes,' he laughed.

Jenna glanced over her shoulder at Sister's office.

'Wayne—'

'Meet me tonight and we'll go for a drink? Eight o'clock?' he persisted.

'Yes, all right,' Jenna said, more to get rid of him than anything.

'When you're quite finished, Nurse Neville, perhaps you can spare a little time from making assignations for your duties here.' The voice was chipped ice; she swung round, red-faced, to confront Tom.

'That's not fair!' she burst out, but got no further as Sister appeared behind him.

'Something wrong, doctor?' Sister looked from Jenna to Tom.

'No, nothing, Sister,' he said smoothly, but his gaze was still on Jenna's face and his eyes were as icy as his voice.

'Sorry, Doc,' Wayne said easily. 'It was my fault. I'll get out of the way.' He raised a cheerful hand to Jenna and went away.

Sister cast a strange look at Tom, and Jenna and was about to say something, then thought better of it and returned to writing up the notes she was busy with when she had heard Tom's voice. Jenna was a good nurse, conscientious and hard-working, she was not one to neglect her work. But she had felt a certain tension between them and she wondered a little.

Jenna lifted her chin and walked past Tom without looking at him. She checked the patient was well wrapped up in the blanket on the trolley and gave the porter the notes for him and helped him manoeuvre the trolley out of the door. When she went out to see to her next patient, Tom had disappeared.

'Telephone for you, Jenna!' Pam called up

the stairs that evening. Jenna had been home only a few minutes.

'Hello, Jenna, I thought I had better give you a ring, we didn't arrange a meeting-place. Shall I pick you up or will you meet me at the "Castle"?'

'Oh, Wayne, I don't ...'

'You're not backing out, are you?' Wayne said, butting in swiftly.

Jenna had been intending to. Then she thought about it; what the heck, she might as well! They had had such good times when they were both in the sixth form; Wayne had shown such promise, he was good-looking and intelligent, taking A-levels and hoping to go to university. But he'd got in with the wrong crowd, didn't put in enough work and failed his exams. Now he seemed to hang around not doing anything special. Perhaps she could influence him to take life more seriously, get a job or study for a career. She could try at least.

'Righto, Wayne,' she said. 'I'll meet you

by the "Castle" in half an hour. Does that suit you?'

'Great!' He sounded really pleased and Jenna felt quite optimistic as she quickly changed into jeans and ran down to the kitchen where Pam was beginning a meal.

'Don't make anything for me, Pam, I'll grab a sandwich. I'm going out.'

'Jenna!' her father called from the lounge. 'What about your dinner? You must eat properly!'

'I've got a sandwich, Dad.' She appeared in the doorway, sandwich in hand, and took a bite. 'I don't want to be late in, I'll have some supper then.'

'Who is it you're going to meet?'

'Just a school-friend, Dad, Wayne Johns.' She hoped he wasn't going to probe any further, and hurriedly picked up her bag from the hall table. 'Sorry! Got to go! See you both later!' Jenna rushed out before he could ask any further questions.

As she walked into the market-square and crossed over to the "Castle", once an old-fashioned pub but now a trendy wine-bar, she began to have doubts. Why on earth should she be able to influence him? Still, she was here now; she had promised to meet Wayne and she would.

He was waiting for her by the entrance. Smiling easily he walked forward to meet her and put an arm casually around her shoulders. 'Right on time, just like the old days, Jenna! You never kept a fellow waiting.' He drew her into the wine-bar. 'What would you like? White wine?'

'Yes. Er, no, make that a spritzer.' Carefully she edged out from under his arm, and waited while he got the drinks.

'Let's find a table, shall we?' Jenna looked around and saw an empty table in the corner. Wayne had shown every indication of standing by the bar, but he shrugged amiably and followed her over.

'What are you doing now, Wayne?' she said as they settled themselves on the red plush seats.

'Nothing much. Dad would like me to

go in with him, but I'm not interested.' Wayne's father was a decorator. 'I'll wait for something more interesting to come along.'

'That might not be so easy, there's not a lot of work going spare in the town at the moment,' commented Jenna

'Then I'll have to move away, won't I?' Wayne grinned. 'But there's no hurry, not for a while yet.'

Jenna took a sip of her spritzer; it was a bit sweet for her taste. 'I don't know, Wayne, maybe if you took a course at the Tech ...'

'Oh, Jenna, you sound like my mother! She's always on at me; I don't need anyone else to tell me what to do!' A quick flash of temper had shown in his eyes, then it was gone and the easy smile returned.

'I can't be bothered anyway; why not have a good time while I can? I didn't come here to talk about boring old work. How are you doing, Jenna You like the work at the hospital?'

Jenna realized she had been unwise to say so much so early. She'd just met him and here she was trying to tell him what to do. Better to leave it for the present.

'I'm in my third year now, and yes, I love the work,' she said, her voice enthusiastic. 'I sit my finals in February. From now until then I'm going to study hard, which is why I wanted to meet you early tonight; I'm going home early to put in an hour before bedtime. If I do that every night I'll be all right.'

'Oh, come on, Jenna.' Wayne moved closer on the seat and took her hand. 'I'm sure you don't need to do that. Why don't you let your hair down for once, we can have a great time! I'll get another drink, for a start.'

'No, Wayne, thanks, I think this will be enough for me. Anyway, it's my shout if you want another.'

'I'm in the money tonight, it's giro day. I'll get them,' he insisted, and giving her hand a squeeze, went to the bar. Jenna sat back and watched him; he was obviously on good terms with the barman, there was some bantering going on as the drinks were poured, both men glancing over to her corner and grinning. She began to feel a little uncomfortable.

'Here you are, a real drink.' Wayne slid onto the seat beside her and put a fresh glass in front of her.

'I haven't finished my first drink,' she said lightly, and he deftly moved her first drink out of the way.

'That's not a real drink!' he said, and picked up her glass. 'Come on, have a sip, it'll do you good!'

Jenna took the glass from him and took a sip to keep the atmosphere light, but she immediately realized it was laced with something strong and put it down on the table.

'No, Wayne, I don't want it. And if you don't mind, I'm going home now.' She stood up and put the strap of her shoulder-bag over her shoulder.

Wayne looked staggered for a minute, then he followed her out of the wine-bar. 'I'm sorry, Jenna, it was just a bit of fun! Come on back, you can have a spritzer if you want one!'

But Jenna was walking off across the market-square. He ran to catch up with her and took her arm, turning her to face him. 'Come on, Jenna! Don't be daft!'

She looked at him and sighed. There really wasn't any harm in him, she thought. But she wasn't going back.

'I'm going home now, Wayne. Like I told you, I have some studying to do.'

'Well, I'll walk home with you. Surely I can do that? We used to be such good friends!'

'All right,' she conceded, and they fell into step side by side. They walked in silence for a while, stepping out briskly as the night was cool.

'Will you come out again?' asked Wayne, as they came to her road.

'I don't think so.'

'I won't do anything so stupid. Come on, Jenna.'

As they reached the gate they had to step to the side for a car coming out of the drive and turning towards town. Wayne took hold of her arm and pulled her in closer to the gatepost protectively. At first they were blinded by the headlights but as the car stopped at the gate before turning she realized with a little start that it was Tom's MG. The car seemed to stay poised for a moment or two as the driver looked straight at them, then it was off, accelerating into town. She gazed after it feeling strangely depressed.

'Who was that?' Wayne was watching her face and had noticed her expression.

'Just a colleague of my father's.' She moved away from his restraining hand. 'Thanks for walking me back. Goodnight, Wayne.' Jenna walked rapidly up the drive.

'I'll give you a ring, shall I?' Wayne called after her, still persisting. Jenna waved her hand non-committedly; she didn't feel like arguing; perhaps by the time he did ring, if he did, she could be firm enough to put him off for good.

'Jenna? Come in here for a moment, will you?' her father called from the lounge, and she put down her bag and went in, flopping down on the sofa beside him.

'Hello, Dad,' she said, giving him a light kiss on the cheek. 'Hi, Pam.' Pam was sitting in her favourite armchair engrossed in a little white jacket she was knitting, or rather she was counting stitches with a frown between her eyebrows and a knitting-needle between her teeth.

Now she took the knitting-needle out of her mouth.

'I saved you some supper. It's on a plate in the fridge, you just have to stick it in the microwave.' Pam smiled at Jenna and went back to her counting.

'Did you say you were going out with Wayne Johns?' said David. 'I thought that was over years ago?'

'We just went for a drink, Dad.'

'He was with that boy who got knocked down on the road on Saturday night, wasn't he? They were drunk, at least the other boy was.'

'Yes, but ...'

'I'm not trying to tell you who you can go out with, Jenna,' David said hastily, seeing her face. 'But be careful, won't you?'

'I told you, Dad, we just went for a drink.' Jenna suddenly realized this didn't sound too good either. 'I only had a spritzer, Dad. And now I'm going to eat my supper and go up and start studying.'

She sensed their concern though, as she heated her supper and ate it at the kitchen table. Why were parents always so over-anxious, she thought rebelliously as she rinsed the plate in the sink, called her goodnights, and ran upstairs to her room.

It was only nine o'clock and she settled down with her books at the little desk in the corner she had had since her schooldays. She would go over operating theatre procedures, she decided; she had to have them at her fingertips as she did the rest of the practical work. Jenna was not too much worried about her written exams, she usually did fairly well on them, but her practical exams did worry her. She knew the work, but when there was anyone watching her, her fingers were all thumbs. So she had planned a strategy whereby she would know the procedures so well they would have become automatic, thus she might manage to keep her self-confidence.

In spite of herself, however, she found it difficult to keep her mind on her work; it strayed away time after time. She wondered what Tom had been doing at the house, Pam hadn't mentioned he was asked to dinner. His face kept getting in between her and her notes, the expression in his deep blue eyes enigmatic. Impatiently she shook her head to free herself of the image, but it was no good. She felt restless and filled with a strange longing for she knew not what.

Five

The lovely weather they had enjoyed for a few weeks of late summer changed as the autumn set in properly in October. It was cold and damp in the mornings when Jenna walked into work, while the leaves were already falling to the ground and turning from the bright hues of autumn to messy, brown heaps on the footpath. She liked the walk to and from work though, and intended to stick to it until the weather turned really bad. Wayne still persisted in meeting her sometimes and often asked her out in spite of her quiet refusals.

Jenna was thinking about Wayne as she changed in the nurses' cloakroom one misty morning. She shivered slightly as she shrugged into her uniform dress, though the radiator was hot as she briefly warmed her hands on it. Maybe she could persuade him to do something useful with his life, she mused absently as she tied up her hair and set her cap on top, fastening it securely with white grips.

'The lists are up on the board.' Elaine came in and hung her coat up in her locker.

'Sorry, what did you say, Elaine? I was miles away.' Jenna satisfied with the set of her cap, smiled at her friend.

'So you were, mind on Dr Yorke, eh?' Elaine grinned; she liked to tease Jenna about Tom since she heard of the Sunday's outing. Jenna frowned at her in mock threat, and she went on hastily, 'Sorry! Anyway, what I was saying was that the transfer lists are out for the student nurses; I noticed as I came by the office.'

'Oh! Did you see where I was going?'

'No, there was a crowd round the board, but if you nip along now you should have time to find out before we report.'

Jenna hurried along the corridor to the

administrator's office and joined the throng around the board. Skimming through the lists she soon came to her own name, J. Neville, third year, Surgical 3. So she only had one more week on Casualty. Oh well, she thought, she liked working on Surgical, though she had really enjoyed Casualty.

Back in the department she reported to Sister Bailey.

'So you're leaving us shortly,' commented Sister. 'Well, I think you have done well here, I shall be submitting a good report. If you should think of taking up casualty work when you have finished your training, I think you would be suitable.'

'Thank you, Sister,' said Jenna gratified. 'Perhaps I will.'

They were interrupted by Sally who put her head around the door.

'Excuse me, Sister, I've just been notified: a baby coming in with severe burns. The ambulance is on its way.'

'Thanks, Sally. Back to work then.' Sister

was once again the brisk and efficient emergency nurse. Swiftly she organized the staff so that when the ambulance arrived there was an empty treatment room waiting with a sterilized burns pack ready. She rang Dr Stelling and now he too was waiting for the arrival of the child.

Jenna and Nurse Foster were detailed to stand by, and in a very short time a trolley with its pathetically small burden was wheeled past the few people with minor injuries waiting in reception. A young woman with uncombed hair and streaming eyes followed the stretcher.

'If you will just sit outside, Doctor will have a look at him.' Jenna took the young woman's arm and sat her down by the entrance to the room. 'Nurse will get you a cup of tea.' She signalled to Jane, who nodded and went off to the kitchen.

'I want to stay with him,' cried the mother.

'So you shall, but just for a moment while they have a look at him, you'll be better off here.' She was firm but kind, and the woman subsided onto the seat, sobbing.

Jenna went into the treatment room where Sister and Dr Stelling were already bending over the little boy who was whimpering softly. She gasped in pity at what she saw; there were third-degree burns to the arms and chest. The boy, who was about a year old, was obviously in shock.

'One for the burns unit at Newcastle.' Dr Stelling straightened and spoke to Sister Bailey, who nodded sadly.

'Poor little mite. I wonder how it happened.'

'No doubt we'll find out from the mother. Meanwhile we'll give him something for the pain and do what we can.'

Later, when the baby had been made as comfortable as possible and was nodding off drowsily with only the occasional snuffling sob, Dr Stelling called in the young mother to discuss how it had happened.

'It was all my fault, doctor,' she said, her face red and guilt-ridden. 'He's been fretful and cross, I think he's cutting a back tooth. I had to make my husband's dinner; I was rocking the pram and cooking at the same time, but he wouldn't go to sleep. Then the chip pan got too hot and I leaned over the pram in a hurry to lift it off the gas ...'

Dr Stelling lifted his head from his notes and glared at her. 'Are you saying you lifted a pan of hot fat across a pram with a baby lying in it?' His tone was cold and censorious, and though it hardly seemed possible the mother's face turned an even deeper shade of red.

'I know,' she said, her voice breaking, 'I know I shouldn't have done it, but it was in the heat of the moment, it was all my fault.'

'Well, it's no good getting upset now,' said Dr Stelling. Jenna's heart ached for the girl; of course she had done a foolish and dangerous thing and the consequences had been dire, but she was shocked and distressed enough, this was entirely the wrong time to have a go at her! Silently she patted the girl's shoulder, trying to instil comfort.

Dr Stelling looked at her impatiently as the girl took her hand and clutched at it; they almost seemed to be ganging up on him.

'I don't think you are needed here now, nurse.' His tone peremptory, he dismissed her with a nod. Jenna gave the shoulder another comforting squeeze before disentangling her hand. She kept her lips firmly together in case she said something she would regret and marched out of the treatment room with her chin in the air.

'Go to lunch, Nurse Neville,' Sister called from the next room. 'You're already ten minutes late.'

'Thank you, Sister.' Jenna collected her cloak and walked out into the fresh air, taking deep gulps of it, cold though it was, in an effort to control her emotions. She was going in to lunch, but as she drew near to the canteen the smell of food nauseated her and she turned abruptly away. She was not really hungry, she decided; she would take a walk in the hospital grounds, she was not in the mood to talk even to her friend Susan.

Jenna did one circuit of the grounds. Though the trees were bare and the ground damp, the sun had come through the clouds and when she came to the sheltered spot between the pathology lab. and the physiotherapy department she sat down on a low wall which skirted a flower-bed and turned her face to the sun. She felt miserable and close to tears.

I really must try not to let the patients' troubles affect me so much, she told herself fiercely, and taking out her handkerchief she blew her nose vigorously. A tear still managed to squeeze itself out of her eye and roll down her cheek. She scrubbed at it, angry with herself now. When she started her night duty on Surgical 3, at least she would be dealing with the pain of adults.

'Nurse Neville? Jenna?'

Jenna jumped at the familiar deep tones, hastily standing up and attempting to control herself; at last she managed to look up into the concerned face of Tom.

'Jenna? What's wrong?' He put out a hand and took her arm.

'Nothing. I'm OK.'

He raised his eyebrows in obvious disbelief, still holding her arm. Jenna was very conscious of him, his masculinity and the compelling attraction he had for her. For one insane moment she had the urge to put her arms around him, to feel his arms around her, protective and comforting. She had to make a physical effort to restrain herself.

'But there is something,' said Tom. 'You are upset.'

'It ... It was that baby, there was a baby, his mother had spilt a chip pan over him

...' Her voice broke as she remembered.

'Oh yes, I heard about it. Jenna you must harden yourself to these things, tragic though they are. We all have to learn that lesson. You are your father's daughter, you know you have to.' He gazed down at her with those disturbing deep blue eyes, understanding and sympathetic. 'You're no good to a patient if you can't control your feelings, Jenna.'

She looked up at him wordlessly. Oh, it was so true, she knew it was true. And she did manage to keep them to herself in front of the patients, she thought privately.

'Have you had lunch?' asked Tom, and she shook her head. 'You had better have some with me then. We can go to the little cafe by the gates.'

'I have to be back in half an hour. Besides, I'm not feeling very hungry.'

'Nonsense,' said Tom. 'You ought to know better than to work on an empty stomach. Just give me a moment to hang up my white coat and get my jacket.'

In the cafe Tom took over completely, ushering her into a booth at the back and ordering omelettes for them both.

'Quick as you can, please, Jack, we have to be back on duty in half an hour.' Tom was obviously a frequent visitor to the place, he was well known to the owner. Jenna was thankful for his thoughtfulness in choosing a secluded booth, she was not really supposed to be out in the town in her uniform, but this place was close to the hospital.

Surprisingly, when the steaming omelettes arrived she found herself tucking into hers with a will, finding it delicious, light and fluffy. Afterwards they even had time to sit back over a cup of coffee. Already she was beginning to feel better.

Tom watched her with a smile. 'I was right, wasn't I? Sometimes all you need to get back on top is a full stomach. Things don't seem too bad now, do they?'

'No. Of course you were right. I was being a bit silly, wasn't I?'

'Better than going the other way—too hard, Jenna.' He leaned over the table and cupped her chin in his hand. 'No sign of distress now. I think you may safely face the rest of the day.' His eyes crinkled at the corners as he smiled; he was very close to her and the intimacy was having a powerful effect on her composure. He knew it too, she realized, as a hint of triumph glowed for a second in his eyes. She glanced at her watch, pinned on the front of her dress, making herself concentrate on the time.

'I must go!' She had only a few moments left of her lunch-hour, she would have to fly. Hastily she fastened her cloak. Sister Bailey was not going to be too pleased if she was late.

They hurried up the drive together. Though they were not touching she was supremely conscious of the man who strode out by her side. At the top of the drive, where their paths diverged as she went on to casualty, he stopped and faced her.

'Are you free on Saturday, Jenna?'

'Yes I am. I start a spell of nights on Monday, so I have Saturday and Sunday free. I must run now though.' She sprinted off, her cloak flying in the stiff breeze.

'I'll ring you at home,' he called after her and watched as she disappeared into the building before striding off towards the surgical side, whistling softly.

The afternoon flew by for Jenna, they were short of a pair of hands as Elaine had gone to Newcastle in the ambulance with the baby and his young mother. But Jenna welcomed the extra work, the time passed all the quicker. She was happy, everything seemed brighter, and there were only minor injuries to deal with.

As she went off duty at five o'clock she decided to try to catch Susan, who was also off that evening. Perhaps they could have a coffee at Rossi's and have a chat, it was a while since they had had time to talk. As it happened, Susan was walking along the corridor, ready to go.

'Fancy calling in at Rossi's for a coffee

and a natter?' Jenna turned and joined her.

'OK. I'm not going anywhere special. Just boring old home!' Susan grinned. 'We won't get so many chances with you on nights. Surgical 3, eh? I saw the notice. I'm going over onto the medical side.'

They walked down the street with their arms linked, and entered Rossi's coffee-shop, where they took their coffee over to a corner table.

'Now!' said Susan. 'Tell me all about it.' She sounded so exactly like she had always done since the days they came into the shop from school that Jenna laughed.

'All about what?'

'Don't you have something to tell me about our dishy Dr Yorke? Come on, I know you have!'

'I don't know what you mean!' Jenna groaned inwardly. The wretched hospital grapevine; someone must have seen them in the cafe at lunchtime.

'Don't give me that, my girl!' said

116

Susan. 'You know very well what I mean. Now then, come clean!'

'Oh, Susan, there's nothing to tell. I was feeling a bit down about the burns case we had this morning, a baby who had to go to Newcastle to the burns unit, and Tom took me to lunch. There was nothing to it; he was feeling sorry for me I suppose, I was being silly.'

'Hmm ... I don't know about that, he came onto the ward this afternoon smiling and whistling to himself as thought he'd just got his FRCS. Then someone had seen you walk up the drive together ...'

'Oh, Susan, you know what it's like in a hospital! If there's nothing to gossip about they'll invent something. He's not really interested in me, it's just because of my father!'

'I think you're interested in him though.' Susan looked knowingly at Jenna's face which had gone quite pink.

'I'm not!' said Jenna lying in her teeth, and took a long drink of coffee then tried to turn the conversation to Susan. 'Anyway, what about you? How are things going with you? You're looking brighter; got over Charles Stelling, have you?'

'I was going to tell you, though I wonder you haven't heard it on the grapevine too! We're going out together again. He told me it didn't mean anything with the others. He likes me.' This last was said defiantly, as she saw the dismay on Jenna's face. 'Don't you say anything about him, Jenna I don't want to hear it.'

Indeed, as Jenna looked at her friend she realized it would be a waste of time to say anything, even the disparaging remark Charles had made to her about nurses. She finished her coffee quietly.

'You're right, it's none of my business. Well, I'll be getting off home. I promised I'd look after Annie tonight and let the parents have a night out.'

'Sorry, Jenna I didn't mean to snap.' Susan had recovered from her bout of irritation and spoke conciliatorily. 'But I'm happy, I don't want to think anything will go wrong. Friends?'

Jenna smiled at her friend, they would always be that. Perhaps Charles Stelling had really fallen for Susan; she hoped it would be all right.

'Friends. Well, I must go, see you tomorrow.' They were at the door of the coffee-shop now and with a cheery wave she went on her way.

'I'll give Annie her bath and get her to bed if you like,' Jenna offered. She was sitting on the lounge carpet with her little sister, they were giving the dolls a tea-party. She poured make-believe milk and tea into the tiny cup and handed it to Annie, who took it carefully and held it to Daisy's lips. Daisy was a large baby doll.

'Drink up now,' said Annie. 'Be a good girl for Mummy,' in a very good imitation of her mother.

'Would you?' said Pam gratefully. 'Then I could go now and have a leisurely bath and shampoo. We're going to the Manor tonight. But there's a casserole in the oven for you.' Pam was looking forward to the night out, and it showed in her happy face. 'You are an angel, looking after Annie for us.'

'Bless her, she doesn't take much looking after. When I've got her nicely tucked up I'll be able to get on with studying. The house will be nice and quiet.'

'You mean without me in it?' grinned Pam. It was true she usually had the radio on and often sang along with it, she had such a sunny, uncomplicated personality, thought Jenna.

'Do have a cake, Jenna.' Annie was impatient with this interruption of their game and was holding out a tiny plate, her little face prim and proper.

'Thank you, dear.' Jenna suppressed a smile. Annie's talking had improved enormously in the last few weeks; she copied Pam all the time.

Later, when Annie was bathed and in

bed, sleepily trying to keep awake as Jenna read her a bedtime story, Pam appeared in the doorway looking smart and pretty in a cerise wool dress with a cowl neckline and swirling skirt.

'She's such a little cherub, isn't she, Jenna?' the fond mother said softly. Jenna nodded her agreement, the baby's dark lashes were fanning out on pink cheeks, in contrast to her fair curls and the white brow. She had lost her battle with sleep and was breathing deeply and evenly. The two women tiptoed out of the room and Jenna closed the door softly.

'My, you do look nice.' Jenna smiled at her stepmother as they went down the stairs. 'Did you get that in Darnton?'

'Fenwicks in Newcastle,' said Pam 'It cost an arm and a leg, but it was worth it.'

She pirouetted in the hall, preening in self-mockery, just as the telephone rang. Pam came to a halt and grimaced.

'Oh Lord, I hope that's not the hospital.

It would be just our luck if David had to go in.'

David had picked up the extension in the kitchen and now he called through to Jenna.

'Jenna! Telephone for you!'

Pam breathed easily again, as David came into the hall looking distinguished and handsome in a well-cut lounge suit. He raised his eyebrows when he saw Pam and whistled softly in admiration.

'You look good enough to eat, my love.' David crossed over and kissed his wife. 'I'm sure we will be the best-looking couple there tonight. Though maybe some people will wonder what a lovely girl like you is doing with an old fuddy-duddy like me!'

Pam laughed softly. 'More likely they'll wonder what a handsome man like you ever saw in an ordinary woman like me.'

'Such a mutual admiration society!' clucked Jenna as she walked into the kitchen and closed the door behind her.

She felt a thrill of anticipation as she picked up the phone, feeling sure that her caller was Tom; he had said he would ring her.

'Hello, Jenna Neville speaking.'

'Jenna? Hi, Jenna, this is Wayne.'

Jenna's heart plummeted; it was quite irrational to feel so let down, but she did.

'Yes, Wayne, what do you want?' she said flatly.

'You don't sound very happy to hear from me.' He sounded reproachful.

'Sorry, Wayne, it's just that I'm busy,' she excused herself.

'I wondered if you were doing anything tonight; we could go for a drink.'

'I can't, Wayne, I'm baby-sitting to-night.'

David put his head around the door. 'We're just off, Jenna See you later!'

'Bye, Dad!' she put her hand over the phone as she spoke. 'Have a good time, both of you.'

'You're on your own then?' There was a different note in Wayne's voice.

'What does that matter? Look, Wayne, I'm going now, I have work to do. Goodnight.'

Firmly, she put the phone back on the hook and began setting a tray for her dinner. It was no good, she was going to have to tell Wayne to leave her alone. Carrying the tray into the lounge she thought again about Tom; how understanding he had been that lunchtime. But that was only because he felt sorry for you, a little voice whispered in the back of her mind. She sighed, and began to eat the slightly dried up casserole.

Jenna was washing up in the kitchen when the doorbell rang, not once as it would normally, but a few times, ending with one long note of impatience. She jumped, and drying her hands quickly on the tea-towel rushed into the hall. She had the presence of mind to put on the chain before opening the door, wondering who it could be making such a noise; Annie would be woken up at this rate.

'Hi, Jenna! I thought I'd come over and keep you company.'

Standing on the step with his feet planted apart as he swayed drunkenly was Wayne Johns, his eyes slightly glazed and his speech slurred.

Six

'What are you doing here?' Jenna hissed at him in exasperation. He was hopeless; whyever had she thought she could help him?

'That's a nice welcome, I must say. Aren't you going to ask me in?'

'I most certainly am not! You've been drinking!' There was a wail from upstairs, the noise had wakened Annie as she had feared. 'You've woken the baby now! Goodnight, I'm going to close the door.'

She slammed the door shut and turned to go up to Annie but as she did so the bell rang again and at the sound Annie's wails grew louder; she was beginning to sound frightened.

Jenna hesitated only for a moment; she could handle Wayne, she told herself.

Taking the chain off the door she opened it.

'Right!' she snapped. 'Sit down there and wait!' She indicated the hall chair. 'I'm going up to see to Annie. Behave yourself until I get back.'

'I always behave myself, darling!' Obediently he lurched to the chair and smiled at her foolishly. Jenna ran up the stairs and picked up the baby, cuddling her close and crooning softly to her.

'There, there, my pet! Nothing is the matter, it was only the doorbell. Go to sleep, my love, Jenna's here.' Gradually Annie's sobs lessened and Jenna dried her eyes and rocked her gently. At last Annie lay back on her pillow, with her thumb in her mouth and her eyes closing. Jenna tucked her in and waited for a moment or two before tiptoeing out and closing the door.

Downstairs she faced Wayne, still sprawling on the hall chair. 'Come into the lounge,' she said shortly. 'We'll wake

Annie in here.' She led the way into the lounge and closed the door.

'Well, you needn't look so disapproving; time was when you were glad to see me!' Wayne was trying to charm her; he had been so used to girls running after him ever since they were at school that he didn't quite believe Jenna wasn't interested, she thought. He sat down on the sofa without being asked and took up his usual sprawling position.

'Wayne, I want you to go. Now. I don't want you to come here again and I don't want to go out with you. Is that clear enough?'

He gazed up at her unsmiling face. 'Oh come on, Jenna, you know you don't mean that! Come and sit down, you know I've always had a soft spot for you.'

'Go! And I mean now.' Jenna still spoke softly but there was a determined note in her voice which seemed at last to get through to him. He sat up straight and the smile slipped slightly.

'It's just a bit of fun, Jenna! I thought me and you could have a cosy time baby-sitting; maybe have a drink or two—'

'Go! Now!'

He didn't choose to hear her. 'You being a nurse and all, I'm sure you can get hold of some stuff; you know what I mean; down at the hospital there must be loads of chances for you. Come on, let your hair down, Jenna don't be such a—'

'Get out!' Jenna's voice rose in furious realization. He was only interested in her because he thought she would have access to drugs! 'You heard me!' She marched to the door and opened it. Wayne looked at her, the smile leaving his face; suddenly he looked ten years older than he was, his face blotched and his eyes red.

'All right! I'm going. I know when I'm not wanted.' Somehow he gathered some shreds of dignity and managed to walk with some deliberation to avoid swaying.

'I don't want to see you, ever again.' Jenna pulled the front door open and waited until he walked past her.

'Well, don't think I cared whether you did or not!' was his parting shot. Jenna watched until he was out of sight then closed and locked the door. She was shaking a little as she went back into the lounge and collapsed into an armchair. Well, at least he hadn't turned really nasty, she thought; she'd managed the situation quite well. But then, he wasn't the type to be violent, he was a gentle boy at school.

Jenna went into the kitchen and made a cup of coffee. How could she have been so stupid as to think she meant anything to him! To think that she might actually be able to change him! Ah well, she had learned a lesson at least; she would steer clear of him in the future. She carried her cup into the lounge and was soon immersed in a textbook, dismissing Wayne from her mind completely.

Jenna soon adapted to night duty, unlike some of her friends who found it difficult to sleep during the day. As a third-year nurse she was often left in charge of the ward, though Night Sister was always within call. On quiet nights she could sit in the ward with its shaded lamp, which was a little pool of light in the darkened ward, showing her reassuring presence if a patient awoke. Of course, quiet nights could be few and far between; there were nights when the only time she sat down was when she went for her break.

'Quite a large list this afternoon,' Day Sister greeted her as Jenna came on duty after her nights off.

'Most of them are comfortable though,' Sister continued. 'We'll go through the report now, then, shall we? Good-evening, nurses.' This last was said as the two junior nurses knocked and entered the office.

'Mrs Scott, bed one, re-section of gut. She's poorly; Ryle's tube to be aspirated hourly—' She carried on down the list of patients operated on that afternoon by Jenna's father, assisted by Dr Yorke.

'Right then, that's the lot,' she said at

last. 'Dr Yorke hasn't been in yet to do his round and write up the medication. No doubt he'll be in shortly.'

Jenna was not surprised; her father had not been back when she had set out for the hospital at seven-thirty that evening.

Jenna was checking on Mrs Scott's drip when she heard the swing doors to the ward close with the slight squeak they always gave, and looking up she saw Tom striding down the corridor into the ward, his white coat flying out behind him. She was getting quite used to the familiar lurch of her heart as she saw his tall, athletic frame, his blond good-looks. Jenna noticed that even the ill patients brightened a little when they saw him, such was his effect on the opposite sex, she thought wryly. Tonight though, he did look tired, though he had a quiet word for everyone before turning to her.

'Hallo, Jenna,' he said, and surely there was a special warmth to his tone. He looked down at her for a long moment, his deep blue gaze darkening, his lips softening into a smile.

'Dr Yorke.' She wondered for an instant why he hadn't asked her out again as he had said he would; had he just said that for something to say? At the thought she wrenched her eyes away. The episode was over in about ten seconds and they were back, doctor and nurse, professionals with patients to see to.

'I'll get the notes then, doctor.' Jenna hurried to the desk and brought over the notes of the patients who had been operated on that day. Tom was bending over Mrs Scott, who was lying supported by pillows; her eyes closed. He checked her TPR and blood-pressure charts and felt her forehead before straightening, obviously satisfied with her progress so far, then went on to the next patient, who had had a cholecystectomy.

'Well, Mrs Brown,' he said. 'At least you'll have no more trouble with your gall-bladder, it's gone now. A nice collection of stones we got too; have you seen them?'

Mrs Brown smiled sleepily. 'I don't know that I want to, doctor; nasty things.'

'I know you don't feel too good just now,' he nodded in understanding, 'but I'll give you something so you can have a good night's sleep and you'll be surprised how soon you'll begin to feel better.'

Jenna handed him her charts and he glanced at them before moving on. She was touched at the trust he seemed to inspire in the patients with his air of friendly efficiency. They moved around the ward, with her unobtrusively anticipating his needs; she watched his strong, brown hands, so gentle with people still sore after surgery.

'I'll write up the notes in the office, nurse,' he said at last. 'Do you mind fetching me a cup of coffee? I'll have the treatment sheets ready for you.'

'Yes, doctor,' said Jenna as formal as he was.

In the background she could hear the

two junior nurses, a second-year student and an auxiliary nurse, chatting to the convalescent patients further down the ward. They had finished the round, in which they straightened sheets and generally made the patients comfortable for the night, but Jenna decided to make the coffee herself.

Ten minutes later she was knocking softly at the office door before taking in the cup of coffee. Tom was sitting at the desk, leaning on his elbows, his head propped on one hand. For one unguarded moment he looked utterly weary and Jenna's heart went out to him. Then he straightened, and running his fingers through his thick blond hair, sat back in the chair.

'Thanks, Jenna. I really need that. Black, I think.' He waved away the cream-jug, and took a long draught of the scalding-hot liquid. 'I've written up the drugs.' He handed her the treatment sheets.

Jenna hesitated for a fraction of a second, hoping he would say something; why he hadn't rung her that weekend as he had said he would. Then she turned to the door, she must get back to the ward.

'Jenna—' he said as she raised her hand to the handle, but she would never know what he was going to say as the door opened at that moment and in came the houseman.

'Oh, sorry, nurse.' The young doctor stood aside to let Jenna out. 'Tom, I'm not happy about—'

Jenna didn't hear any more as she closed the door quietly and went to lay out the drugs for Sister to check. Night Sister would be doing her rounds in a few minutes.

It was a very weary Jenna who left the hospital next morning and walked to the bus shelter. It was a cold, damp morning with a chill wind which had a hint of snow in it. She shivered as she buried her chin in her scarf and looked hopefully up the road for any sign of the bus.

It had been one of those nights when everything seemed to happen; not one, but two emergency admissions with acute appendicitis; Jenna's auxiliary nurse having to relieve on the medical side as flu had struck half the staff down; and besides all this the need to keep the post-operative patients under close observation. The poor houseman hadn't managed to get to bed at all, and he had a normal day to face.

At least, thought Jenna we have day staff relieving us.

Her ears began to tingle with the cold and she held her mittened hands over them. At last the town service-bus rumbled along and she climbed thankfully aboard—the journey wasn't all that long, but she didn't feel up to walking against the wind. She settled down in a window seat, enjoying the muggy warmth. Immediately her sleepy mind turned to thoughts of Tom.

Of course he too had been called out again during the night, as indeed her father had been. Since she had been working on

Surgical 3, she often saw Tom on the ward. He was always polite but a little impersonal with her, though even on the busy ward there were moments when they could have had a personal word. No, obviously he had lost interest in her, if he ever had been interested, that is.

Her mind returned to the night she had seen him in the Manor Hotel with his beautiful dinner companion. Of course that was the reason. She stared at the image looking back at her mistily through the window. It wasn't bad, she supposed, but nothing special. Critically she judged her nose, too short; her mouth, too full. It was an ordinary face with ordinary brown eyes and hair. Not to compare at all with that vision Tom had been out with. Jenna's self-esteem sank even lower; she sighed heavily as she alighted from the bus at the end of her road.

A sense of the ridiculous affected her as she walked up the drive and she grinned to herself. She really was putting herself down; it was because she was so tired. If Tom didn't want her, then she certainly didn't want him! She opened the door and a heavenly smell of bacon and eggs wafted through to her. She could hear David and Pam chatting quietly in the dining-room as she hung up her coat. It would be nice to have a family meal all together for a change.

'Morning, all,' said Jenna as she went in. 'Though it's not a very nice morning, cold and wet.' She shivered as she walked over to the radiator and warmed her hands.

'Morning, love.' David smiled at her in sympathy. 'You've had a hard night, I suppose. We're pretty busy on surgical just now. Comes in waves, doesn't it?'

'It certainly does.' Jenna spoke with feeling. 'Gosh, I'm ravenous, Pam!' Pam was lifting Annie from her high chair.

'I've cooked you some sausages besides the bacon and eggs; I never know just what to give you in the mornings. I suppose really it should be dinner.'

'Lord no, I couldn't face dinner!' Jenna bent over and kissed Annie on the top of the head. 'Morning, my poppet! What are you going to do today?'

'Me go to school!' Annie said proudly. She had recently started going to nursery school and loved it; being a gregarious child like her mother, it was the company of other children which she loved best.

'I'll get your breakfast, it's all ready,' said Pam.

'Don't bother. You see to Annie. After all, she mustn't be late!'

Jenna tucked into her meal with a will, while David lifted his morning paper and looked through it while he drank his coffee. The front door closed behind Pam and Annie. The dining-room was warm and comfortable and father and daughter sat in silent companionship while she finished her breakfast and he read his paper. But when she put down her knife and fork he folded his paper and cleared his throat. Jenna looked at him enquiringly.

'Something up, Dad?'

'You know, Jenna, I'm not the old-fashioned type who lays the law down about who you should see or not see, I know you're a sensible girl—'

Jenna was taken aback, this sort of thing had never come up between them before. 'What on earth are you on about, Dad?' She sat back in her chair and grinned at him.

'Well, what I mean is, you're not getting involved with Wayne Johns, are you? I don't want to play the heavy father, but you know he runs around with a bad crowd. That friend of his we had in the other week, it wasn't only drink, there was some suspicion of drugs with him.' David looked at her anxiously, he was trying to pick his words carefully.

'You mean you don't trust me any more?' Jenna was upset and dismayed that he should feel it necessary to speak like this. He had always trusted her completely before.

'No, Jenna of course I trust you; as I said, you are a level-headed young lady. But I know you've been seeing him, and I know that crowd he is running around with.'

'As it happens, I have stopped seeing him,' Jenna said with dignity. 'I only really went out with him once.'

'I've seen him myself, hanging around the hospital waiting for you, Jenna, while you were still on day duty. And Tom said—'

'Tom said what?' Jenna sat up straight as though she had been struck. 'You mean Tom Yorke?'

David looked a bit embarrassed. 'It was that night you looked after Annie when we went out to dinner. Tom said he saw you let Wayne out of the house. Now, what was he doing here?'

'How dare he?' Jenna was beginning to feel really angry now. 'What right has Tom Yorke to go snooping around me? Just who does he think he is?'

'Now, Jenna he was genuinely concerned. And he wasn't snooping, he was simply going past the house.'

'Simply going past! I'll bet!'

'You've got to admit, Jenna, you didn't mention to us that Wayne was here that night,' David said quietly.

Jenna slumped in her chair; suddenly she was unbearably weary. 'Oh Dad, there was nothing to tell. Wayne called to ask me out and I told him I didn't want to know. I know he isn't the boy he used to be when we were at school. Annie woke up and I had to see to her so I asked him to wait in the hall. That's all there was to it. And I still think Tom Yorke had no business telling you; it's my life and it's nothing to do with him. Now I'm tired and I'm going to bed.'

Jenna stood up and went out of the room, going straight upstairs to her room, leaving David with the feeling that he had handled the situation rather badly.

Jenna lay in bed with the duvet tucked

cosily around her, the curtains drawn against the winter's day, creating a grey half-light in the bedroom. Usually she was able to go straight off to sleep, especially after a busy night, but today thoughts were buzzing around in her head.

She thought about taking a room nearer the hospital until after she sat her finals; then she intended going to Newcastle to do her midders anyway, if possible at the Princess Mary's Maternity Hospital. In the meanwhile, if she had her own place she could preserve her independence; after all she was nearly twenty-one.

Indignation at Tom welled up in her; impatiently she turned over and thumped her pillow into a ball, half wishing it was Tom's head. 'He's not interested in me; what right has he to interfere in my life!' she mumbled into the poor abused pillow.

Gradually, however, the anger and indignation gave way to sadness and that little ache somewhere inside her which only seemed to come when she thought about Tom. His face seemed imprinted on her eyelids when she closed her eyes, his eyes dark and tender as they had been that day in the little wooded ghyll on the high moor, the sunlight glinting on his hair, a golden god. And she knew she only wished he did have some say in her life.

'Fool!' Jenna spoke aloud, fiercely; what was the point in wishing for the moon? She was tired, that was the problem, everything would look different once she'd had a good sleep. She tried to put it all out of her mind, determined not to spend a wakeful day, and eventually her youth and good health combined with her tiredness and she dropped into a deep, dreamless sleep.

When she came down the stairs that evening, refreshed and ready to face another night on duty, her natural good spirits had replaced her depression.

David looked up at her quizzically as she entered the lounge. Father and daughter were very close and neither liked to be at odds with the other.

'I'm sorry, Jenna,' he said simply. 'I trust you to be sensible, of course. And you are perfectly well able to choose your own friends, you are old enough now. I suppose it's just that I still think of you as not much older than Annie.' He smiled ruefully.

'Oh Dad, I'm sorry too.' Jenna dropped a kiss on his head. 'But it was the idea of Tom spying on me, then having the gall to tell you. Anyone would think Victoria was still on the throne!'

'I don't think he meant it like that,' said David. 'He does go past the house, he lives just up the road now. He was only passing a remark; for all he knew Pam and I were home that night. I just told you badly, that's all.'

'Hmm,' said Jenna but she was not really convinced. Things hadn't been the same since that man came to Darnton, though why that should be she couldn't think.

'Evening, Jenna did you sleep well?'

Pam came in from the kitchen, smiling in relief when she saw the tension had eased between her husband and step-daughter. Jenna saw that Pam must have had a diplomatic word with David; she was sensible and straightforward. Jenna didn't mind at all, Pam was a good friend as well as her stepmother. Her sunny nature was good for them all. And after all, she didn't really want to leave home, not until she had passed her finals. *If* she passed her finals, she reminded herself.

Seven

During the next few nights on the ward Jenna didn't see anything of Tom and presumed he was taking the time off due to him. She would have liked to ask her father but did not in case he should think she was interested in Tom's doings, which of course she was not, she told herself.

The nights were fairly busy and during the quiet times she was able to study at the desk in the middle of the ward. So, all in all, her spell of night duty was going over quite well. Jenna was not one to bear a grudge and her anger at Tom was almost forgotten when he turned up on the ward one evening in place of the houseman to do an evening round.

'Good-evening, Nurse Neville.' The deep-timbred masculine voice sent a shock wave coursing through Jenna's veins, and she dropped the thermometer in its holder with a slight plop and picked up the temperature chart quickly to hide the sudden trembling in her hands. The man in the bed looked at her curiously, surely his temperature hadn't gone up enough to cause this pretty nurse's discomposure?

Jenna found her voice. 'Evening, Dr Yorke.' She managed to look calmly at him. 'I won't be a moment. Your temperature's normal, Mr Teesdale.' She smiled at the middle-aged man in the bed, who decided regretfully that it must the handsome blond-haired doctor who was the cause of her heightened colour. Well, at least he felt well enough to regret it wasn't him.

'There are just one or two things I want to see you about,' said Tom, as they walked down the ward.

'There are one or two things I want to see you about.' Jenna spoke just above a whisper, not even realizing she had spoken aloud, she was remembering how angry she had been.

'What did you say?' They had reached the office by this time and Tom raised his eyebrows. Jenna went in and laid out the case-notes of the post-operative patients on the desk.

'I understand you have been discussing my choice of friends with my father?' It was entirely the wrong place for her to bring it up and she knew it quite well, but it was boiling on the end of her tongue.

'What?' Tom looked genuinely startled.

'Dad said you told him Wayne Johns was at the house whilst he and Pam were out.'

'*I* did?'

'Yes, *you* did.' Jenna lifted her chin pugnaciously. Now she had brought it up they might as well have it out. But Tom had other ideas.

'I don't think this is a subject for discussion on the ward, Jenna.' His voice was mild but decisive. 'We will arrange to meet when we are both off duty, shall we?'

Jenna blushed; he was right of course, this was no place to squabble. 'My nights off start tomorrow as it happens, but I don't think it's a good idea to meet.' She bit her lip and looked down at her shoes. 'I'm sorry, I shouldn't have brought it up on the ward.'

'Well, it's up to you. If you can't bear to see me off duty it's entirely your decision.' Tom turned dismissively to the notes. 'I can manage now, nurse, you can go back to your work.'

Jenna was left to return to the ward feeling she had managed the encounter very badly indeed. She helped settle the patients down for the night and dimmed the lights before sitting at the desk and taking out her books. Gradually the ward became quiet and her junior went off to supper. She hadn't heard Tom leave the ward but presumed he must have done while she was busy.

Jenna tried to concentrate on her notes on surgical procedures, but found herself returning time after time to the same paragraph without even turning the page. Exasperated with herself she put down the folder and began one of her frequent walks round the ward, checking on the patients, having a quiet word with Mr Teesdale who was having difficulty in getting to sleep.

'It's all right, nurse,' he replied to her enquiry. 'I'm not in any pain, just a bit wakeful that's all.'

'I'll make you some cocoa, shall I?' she offered.

'That would be nice.'

Jenna had a last look at the other beds, where everything seemed peaceful, and went swiftly into the kitchen and put on milk for the cocoa.

'Make an extra cup for me while you're about it, please?' Jenna jumped as she heard Tom's voice from the doorway. He was standing leaning against the door jamb watching her as she spooned cocoa into the cup and mixed it into a smooth paste with a little cold milk. There was a slight frown between his brows, a brooding in his eyes.

'Yes of course, doctor.' Jenna turned to the fridge for more milk, then took down another cup.

'If you really won't meet me I'll walk along to supper with you when your relief turns up,' Tom said firmly. 'I really think we should have this out, don't you?' He stood aside while she took Mr Teesdale his cocoa. She looked at him directly but didn't answer until she had returned and handed him his own cup.

'All right,' she decided with some reluctance. 'I can meet you tomorrow. If you were to walk me to the canteen at this time of night it would be all over the hospital grapevine by tomorrow! But that's the only reason!' she added hastily.

Tom's face was bland and enigmatic. Though he knew as well as she did what hospital gossip was like, she thought hotly.

'There's no need to look so fiery about it. I'm suggesting a date for dinner, that's all.' He drank his cocoa in one long draught, his deep blue eyes looking over the rim of the cup with some amusement at her.

'Dinner!' Jenna exclaimed, and would have gone further, but at that moment the main door to the ward opened and she heard Sister's footsteps coming up the corridor.

'Eight o'clock. I'll pick you up.' Tom put down his cup and swung off down the corridor. ''Evening, Sister!' she heard him say as he went. Jenna was left fuming; high-handed wasn't the word for him!

'Good man that,' remarked Night Sister, looking thoughtfully after him. 'Nothing wrong I hope? Or was he doing a routine round?'

'No, nothing wrong,' Jenna replied. 'Do you want to see the report?'

'We'll just go round, shall we?' Sister was already marching into the ward, her watchful gaze falling on everything. 'I've seen a copy in the office. Everyone seems to be asleep and comfortable, nurse.' She nodded in satisfaction, before going on her way.

Susan was having supper when Jenna entered the canteen and she waved and moved over to make room for her friend.

'Hi, Jenna! How are you doing?' Susan sounded happy and cheerful; things must be going well for her, thought Jenna.

'Oh, all right.' Jenna looked down at the liver and bacon and mashed potatoes on her plate. It didn't look very appetizing, but nevertheless she picked up her knife and fork and began eating methodically. By this time she was used to hospital food.

Susan was almost finished clearing her plate, she had a healthy appetite. She took a last forkful of mashed potato and sat back, smiling at Jenna.

'Now,' she said. 'Tell me all about your love-life.'

Jenna swallowed a piece of overdone liver and grinned. 'What love life is that then?' she said tolerantly. 'I haven't got one at the moment.'

Susan raised her eyebrows. 'No? What about Dr—' The warning glance from Jenna made her cut short. 'OK, I'm not saying anything. I'll tell you about mine instead.' The smile left her eyes and she stirred her coffee. Jenna was puzzled, Susan had seemed so happy only a moment before.

'I thought Charlie and you were back together and everything in the garden was rosy?' she said in some surprise.

'Oh yes, it is,' Susan said quickly. 'I know you're sceptical, Jenna but this time he really is different. He's sweet and attentive and never looks at another woman.'

Jenna managed to keep her thoughts out of her expression, though a quick flash of Charlie flirting with the nurse in casualty rose before her.

'Anyway I love him.' Susan picked up her spoon and attacked her bowl of rice-pudding and raisins, as though that settled everything.

'But there is something bothering you,' Jenna persisted.

Susan sighed and put down her spoon. She glanced around the room before replying. There were only a few nurses scattered around the tables eating supper, and no-one near enough to hear what they said.

'I wasn't going to tell you, I know you don't like him much. But like I said, I'm crazy about him, and I think he loves me; he's just not one to commit himself straightaway.' She stared at her friend, challenging her to comment. Jenna held her tongue with some difficulty.

'He's asked me to go away with him next weekend, our nights off coincide. Oh Jenna we are going to fly to Paris!' Romantic excitement shone in her eyes.

'Paris!'

At Jenna's exclamation Susan flushed slightly. 'Why not? I've never been to France. Flying from Newcastle it doesn't take so long. Plenty of time in three days.'

'Yes of course, but—' Jenna looked at Susan helplessly; what could she say that wouldn't make her sound hopelessly old-fashioned? And what girl in love could refuse a weekend in Paris with her beloved? Jenna looked down at the congealing gravy on her plate and stirred it moodily into the scoop of mashed potato.

'You might at least be pleased for me!' said Susan.

'Oh yes, it will be lovely to have a trip to Paris,' Jenna said quickly. 'I *am* pleased for you, Susan; I was taken by surprise, that's all. I hope you have a lovely time!'

Susan's tone softened. 'Oh, I know, Jenna I know you just don't want me to be hurt. But really, it's OK; I have some money saved what with not having a holiday last year; I am paying my own way. And who knows, in the romantic atmosphere of Paris anything could happen!'

'Yes, that's what I mean,' Jenna couldn't stop herself from remarking.

Susan stood up abruptly. 'I meant, we might get engaged,' she said shortly. 'I have to get back to work now.' Her eyes sparkled and the flush had returned to her plump cheeks.

'Yes, of course.' Jenna stood also. 'Oh Susan, I didn't mean to upset you. I just wish you all the best; I'm sure it will turn out all right.' She looked anxiously at her friend; she didn't want them to part with bad feeling between them.

'It's not like you think, Jenna really it isn't.' Susan softened. 'Oh, I know you're thinking of me, but I am a big girl now, I can look after myself.'

'Yes, I know. And I hope you have a good time and everything turns out right.'

'It will. Oh, it'll be great, Jenna.' Talking

about the trip seemed to make Susan forget any doubts she had had, her eyes were bright with anticipation. It would be a shame to say any more and put a damper on her, Jenna thought. She pushed aside her plate and had a sip of tea before she too prepared to go.

'I may as well go back with you some of the way,' she said. 'I'm not hungry anyway.'

The two girls walked together as far as the point where Susan turned off for the medical side.

'Well, have a good time, if I don't see you before you go.' Jenna waved to her friend and set off at a brisk pace for the ward. People had their own lives to live, she reflected, it was silly to interfere and never did any good. Ruefully she thought of Wayne as well as Susan; both would work things out for themselves. And after all, she wasn't exactly making a great success of her own life at the present time!

Her thoughts returned to Tom; lately he seemed to be on her mind most of the time. She would go to dinner with him tomorrow; she would keep her head with him and tell him coolly where he got off. Now she determined to put him out of her mind and concentrate on her work. He was just another registrar of her father's and before long he would gain his FRCS and go on his way to take up a consultancy somewhere else, where no doubt he would cause some heart-fluttering among other nurses.

Next morning Jenna walked along the High Street on her way home, looking in boutique windows. She was newly paid and had a vague idea of buying herself something, a new dress or even a full outfit. Not for anything would she admit to herself that she wanted something new to wear that evening when she was out with Tom; no, she needed a new outfit, it was getting on for Christmas and there would be parties and outings.

Jenna was just beginning to think she was not going to see what she wanted, the morning was bright but cold and she was tired and starting to feel the effects of the icy wind. She was almost to the end of the line of shops and was thinking she might as well go home to bed for a few hours. Jenna never spent the whole day in bed when it was her night off, but needed a couple of hours at least.

She almost didn't look in the last window and was turning for home when she saw it. An elegantly draped dress in muted tones of green and lavender in a soft wool.

She perked up immediately and went in, praying it would be the right size, but without much hope, most things turned out to be too large for her her.

'It looks like it was made for you, madam!' the salesgirl cooed, as no doubt she did to everyone, thought Jenna cynically. But she had to admit, as she swirled round before the long mirror, it did fit her perfectly; it even looked good with her flat-heeled working-shoes. The colours seemed to complement her own colouring, her hair combed hastily loose, lying lustrously dark against her white skin, her velvet-brown eyes glowing brightly despite her fatigue.

Jenna did some quick calculations in her head. The dress cost an arm and a leg, but she had shoes which matched it at home which were hardly worn, and if she was careful with her money for a month—

'I'll take it,' she said. Though her heart beat a little faster as she wrote out the cheque, and walked home with the carrier bag containing the precious dress.

'You're a bit late this morning. Had a hard night?' Pam asked sympathetically as Jenna went in. Then she noticed the carrier from the most exclusive shop in town. 'Oh, been shopping I see! Some special date, is it?'

'No, nothing like that,' avowed Jenna. 'But Christmas is coming, and I will need something to wear to parties and things.'

Pam nodded and forebore to mention that there were some weeks to go to Christmas yet. 'Can I have a look at it then?' She peered curiously into the paper bag. 'Oh I say, the colour is gorgeous!'

'It is, isn't it.' Jenna was gratified. 'You'll see it on tonight, I'm going out to dinner. Just now I think I'll just have some cornflakes, Pam then I'll go to bed till lunchtime, and get up for the afternoon.'

'You should eat a proper breakfast,' reproved Pam. 'I could soon whip you up some scrambled eggs at least.' There was a speculative look in her eyes but she refrained from asking about Jenna's dinner date, though she was sure that it was the real reason for Jenna's new dress.

'Just cornflakes, I'll eat lunch.' Jenna had not missed the look in Pam's eyes; she could see Pam was dying to know who she was going out to dinner with. 'It's Tom Yorke,' she said; after all, Pam would find out when he called that evening. 'Don't read anything into it though, there's nothing like that between us.'

'Like what?' Pam asked innocently, then had to grin. 'Well, you never know, do you? There's plenty of time and you must admit he's gorgeous!'

'I don't think he's so attractive,' Jenna said loftily. 'Too self-opinionated really.'

'Then why buy such an expensive dress?' Pam was disbelieving.

'I told you, it's for Christmas!' But she could see she was fighting a losing battle so she shrugged her shoulders and went to get her bowl of cornflakes.

Jenna woke feeling quite refreshed and spent a lazy afternoon playing with Annie and gossiping with Pam who had wisely given up the subject of Tom. David came in and they had a cosy family tea by the fire, with toasted teacakes oozing with butter, and chocolate cake. David and Jenna were lucky in that they could eat what they wanted without it affecting their weight; Pam just didn't bother too much, she enjoyed her food.

'Well, I'll go up and wash my hair and have a long, leisurely bath, I think.' Jenna stood up and stretched lazily, after licking chocolate cream off her fingers.

'Going out?' David sat back in his chair and looked up at her.

'I have a dinner date, Tom's calling at eight.'

'As it's only five o'clock I should think you have loads of time to get ready then.' David looked amused.

One of the drawbacks of living at home, reflected Jenna as she ran the bath and put in a generous supply of her favourite bath-oil. The family knew every little detail of your life. She climbed into the steaming water and lay back luxuriously. On the other hand, she mused, there were great compensations.

By a quarter to eight Jenna was slipping the dress over her head. She looked it over carefully in the mirror; she had been right, it was such a perfect fit; it draped from one shoulder in soft folds to the tiny nipped-in waist, from which it flared slightly to her knees. Usually she had to have her dresses shortened, but this one seemed made for her. She had been right too about the green shoes, they were just the right colour and she had a bag to match them.

Glancing at the clock Jenna saw it was almost eight, though she hadn't yet heard the bell. Plenty of time to do her face and hair, she decided, so what if he had to wait! When at last she was satisfied with her reflection in the mirror she still hadn't heard the front door bell. But she was used to doctors not being on time, quite often her father had been late through some emergency, so she supposed Tom had been delayed. She would go down and wait in the lounge.

Jenna could hear Pam and little Annie having a splashing time in the bathroom, so she opened the door and did a little pirouette to show off her dress. Both Pam and Annie looked at her with genuine admiration.

'Pretty Jenna!' pronounced Annie from under a layer of bubbles.

'Whew! I'll say!' Pam pushed back a stray lock of sandy hair with a hand holding a soapy sponge, and sat back on her heels. 'It's lovely, Jenna you look a treat.'

'Well thank you kindly.' Jenna blew Annie a kiss. 'See you tomorrow, my poppet. Sweet dreams!'

She felt great as she went downstairs, their admiration had done wonders for her ego. And she couldn't help a small thrill of anticipation at the thought of going out with Tom again, in spite of the real reason for the date. She was smiling happily as she opened the door of the lounge and swung round for her father's benefit.

'Tra-la!' she sang, and executed a slight curtsey.

'Tra la indeed!' Jenna stopped abruptly at the sound, the smile slipping slightly. There in the comfortable chair by the fire sprawled the long-legged length of Tom, his fair hair gleaming in the firelight, his eyes blue-black and gleaming. David was pouring sherry at the sideboard, but he turned around and whistled his appreciation.

'I don't mind you being a bit late if this is the result,' said Tom as he unfurled himself out of the chair and stood up. His eyes ran over her slowly, approving every detail. Jenna blushed slightly under his gaze, and to cover up turned to her father and accepted a glass of the pale amber liquid.

'Where are you thinking of going?' asked David, as he settled down on the sofa. 'The Manor, I suppose?'

'No, as a matter of fact. I thought we would drive out into the country and I booked a table at the Jersey Cow.'

'Well, at least it's not foggy. Quite a good night for driving up to Barney.'

'Barney?'

'The local name for Barnard Castle; haven't you heard it yet?' Jenna put in lightly, her composure restored. She sat down beside her father on the sofa and looked up at Tom over the rim of her glass.

'Better get along then,' David sighed theatrically. 'I daresay Fletcher and I can cope if an emergency comes in.' Fletcher was the young houseman; if necessary he would get straight on to David during Tom's night off.

It was warm and cosy in the little two-seater as they drove up the country road into Teesdale. Jenna snuggled her chin into the warmth of her fur jacket and gazed ahead at the frost-laden branches of the trees by the roadside, looming ghostly white in the headlights. Tom, after glancing at her enigmatically, spoke little and kept his attention on the road ahead.

The restaurant was fairly busy but Tom and Jenna were soon seated at a table in the corner favourably situated away from the smells of the kitchen. Tom had the sort of presence which got what he wanted without any effort; waiters seemed to catch his eye immediately.

'I think we will wait to have our talk after we have eaten, don't you agree?' Tom spoke smoothly.

Jenna bowed her head and studied the menu. She had been going over in her mind what she would say to him while they had been travelling up in the car, preparing a few choice and cutting remarks. He must have been watching her, it was almost as though he could read her mind!

'Ready to order, sir?' The waiter was back and Jenna realized she hadn't even seen what was on the menu, she had been looking at it blindly. She glanced down quickly and picked the first thing she saw.

'Oh, soup, I think. And the duckling.'

'Yes, I'll have the same.' As Tom handed the menus to the waiter his attention was taken by a girl standing in the entrance. Curious, Jenna followed his gaze. Walking towards them with a lithe grace was the golden-haired, beautiful woman Jenna had seen with him at the Manor.

'Tom! Darling!' she said, and as he stood courteously she kissed him with enthusiasm, before turning a brilliant blue gaze on Jenna. 'Who's your little friend?'

Eight

'Hello there, Tom; and Nurse Neville, would you believe!'

The polite smile slid from Jenna's face as she saw Charlie Stelling behind the woman. So much for his changed ways, she thought in the split second before Tom intervened.

'Jenna, this is Diane Woodford. And of course you know Dr Stelling. Diane, Jenna Neville. I didn't know you were back in the north, Diane?'

'Oh, a nurse!' Diane managed to make the term sound slightly disparaging, and Jenna began to fume inwardly. Diane gave her a brief smile before turning back to Tom and laying a hand on his arm. 'I was in Durham on business so I thought I'd spend a few days in Darnton. I called,

but there was no reply. Now I see why!'
She glanced back over at Jenna

'So she had to make do with me, old
chap. That's what cousins are for!' Stelling
grinned fondly at Diane. 'Not that I mind,
it's a pleasure.'

So she was Charlie's cousin, Jenna had
time to think, before she realized with
dismay that Diane was proposing that they
join together in a foursome.

'Perhaps not tonight,' Tom said. 'Jenna
and I have things to discuss.' His tone was
firm, almost dismissive, and Diane's lips
tightened briefly.

'That's OK. We quite understand,' said
Charlie a knowing look appearing on his
face. 'Come along, Diane, our table's
waiting.' He took her hand from Tom's
arm and led her away.

Jenna was feeling thoroughly ruffled and
it showed in her heightened colour and the
angry sparkle in her eyes. Watching her,
the corners of Tom's mouth twitched; he
covered it with the corner of his napkin

as the waiter placed the soup before them. Jenna picked up her spoon aggressively.

'What's so funny?' she demanded fiercely. 'You think I should like being talked down to?'

Tom put on a straight face. 'I'm sure Diane didn't mean anything,' he said in soothing tones. 'She doesn't always think before she speaks, that's all.' He tasted his soup, a country vegetable, home-made and delicious.

'Come on, eat your dinner,' he ordered.

Jenna opened her mouth to retort then thought better of it and did as she was bid. She had had little to eat all day and the smell of the soup made her realize she was ravenous. The meal was delicious, the duckling cooked to perfection, the wine just right, so that when they finally sat back over their coffee she was feeling mellowed, and her anger, usually short-lived, had deserted her. Tom confined himself to small-talk over dinner, proving yet again what a charming companion he could be when he put himself out. Jenna noticed Diane often shot a look in the direction of their table, but Tom acted as though he and Jenna were the only persons in the room.

'Charlie Stelling seems very taken with his cousin,' Jenna found herself remarking. 'Kissing cousins, I think.'

'Yes. Well, she is a very beautiful girl.' Tom didn't even glance over at Diane and Charlie. He was watching Jenna intently, and there was something deep in his eyes which made her tremble slightly. But a silly pang went through her when he described Diane as a beautiful girl, even in such an offhand manner.

Tom leaned over the table and covered her small hand with his, the long brown surgeon's fingers caressing hers lightly. Her eyes were drawn to his as though by a magnet; she felt she was drowning in the blue depths of his gaze.

'Did I tell you how beautiful you look tonight, Jenna?' His voice was low and vibrant; she felt alone on an island amidst that crowded room, quite alone with him.

'I ... I ...' Her mind fluttered feebly against the spell of him, and instantly he released her hand and sat back in his chair. When he raised his hand to the waiter for the bill he seemed to have retreated behind an impersonal front and she felt an irrational sense of loss.

'I haven't forgotten why you are here,' said Tom. 'We need to have a talk to get some things straightened out.' He glanced around the room. 'I think this is not the place though. Shall we go back to my rooms?'

'I don't—'

'For goodness sake, Jenna! I'm not about to ravish you! I just think we would be better by ourselves, and my rooms are the only place I can think of.'

Jenna flushed and nodded her agreement; after all it would be easier to talk if they were on their own. At least she wouldn't be feeling the eyes of the lovely

Diane on her. As they went out to the car it occurred to her that it could also be the reason why Tom wanted to get away, and the thought was not comforting.

Tom drove quickly back into Darnton, threading his way expertly through the late-night traffic of the town, passing Jenna's home and going on down the road to a newly-built block of service flats. He was quiet all the way until he opened the door to his own apartment, leading into what was obviously a bachelor's home with deep leather armchairs and plain brown carpet.

'I'll take your coat,' he said. 'Now, come and sit down and tell me exactly what it is that I have done to upset you.' He led her to the sofa and sat down beside her, still holding onto her hand.

For a minute Jenna was at a loss to remember what it was she wanted to say to him; being so close to him and feeling his masculine magnetism wash over her was driving any other thought from her head.

'Well?' Just for a second she saw a flicker

of amusement at the back of his eye and with an effort of will she sat very straight and practically wrenched her hand away.

'You were spying on me!' she said at last, and even in her own ears it sounded childish.

'I was?'

'What business is it of yours if Wayne Johns was at the house? He's an old school-friend and I have a perfect right to see him!'

'Yes, of course.' Tom spoke calmly and smoothly.

'Then why did you think you should tell my father?' she demanded hotly.

'I simply mentioned I saw him as I came past,' Tom said reasonably. 'I was not spying on you at all. Not really.'

'What do you mean, not really?'

'Well, that young man is not the type you should be getting mixed up with, Jenna. It's easy to see that crowd will be in serious trouble if they go on the way they are doing; already we've had a couple of them casualties in the hospital.'

'You insufferable prig! What right have you to pass judgement?' Jenna's temper was rising; she turned blazing eyes on Tom. 'And what you mean is you really were spying, weren't you?' Jenna started up from the couch and looked around for her jacket. 'I'm going home; you don't need to come, I'll walk!'

Tom's face was set and hard as he stood and caught hold of her shoulders, bringing her round to face him and holding her hard against him so that her head fell back and she had to look up to him. His nostrils flared; he was white around the mouth under his tan.

'You little fool!' He glared at her. 'Or is it that you just don't care? You like to have men dancing after you, don't you? Oh, I could see how you didn't like to see Charlie with Diane tonight! But you're playing with fire when you mess about with that crowd! And you must know it was because I was interested that I noticed you

182

with Johns!' His face was only inches away from hers, his eyes bored into her eyes with an intensity which held her motionless for a long second before his mouth descended on her lips, hard and relentless.

Jenna felt herself lifted in arms like steel bands; the tide of his passion swept her along, she was unable to resist. Indeed, the response of her own body took her by complete surprise; she moaned softly as her arms crept around his neck and they sank to the couch.

It was Tom who lifted his head at last, looking down at her softly parted lips, the black lashes fanned against her flushed cheeks. His hand was on her breast, the nipple strained against the soft wool of her dress as it hardened in excited response. Jenna's eyes opened as he lifted his head, the expression in her velvety brown eyes languorous and inviting. She felt unable to resist him, his magnetic attraction.

Tom sat up straight, holding her away from him; a shutter seemed to fall over his eyes and he was in complete control of himself.

'I think I had better take you home,' Tom said, in a dry level voice, quite without emotion.

'What?' Jenna gasped, unable to take in his words or the abrupt change in him. She was trembling with the intensity of her emotions, on the verge of tears.

'I'll get your coat.' Tom stood up as she desperately tried to pull herself together. Shakily she got to her feet; catching a glimpse of herself in the wall-mirror she saw that a long strand of waving hair had come loose from her slide. Hastily she tried to tidy it with her hands then pulled her dress straight, as Tom came back with her jacket and held it for her to put on. Jenna snatched it from him and pulled it on furiously, causing Tom's lips to lift at the corners. Jenna was furious all right; furious at her traitorous emotions for betraying her like that, furious at her body for its throbbing response to him, but most of all furious with Tom; she was becoming convinced he was playing with her. She couldn't speak, she couldn't even look at him. Turning to the door she rushed blindly out.

'Hang on a minute!' As she reached the front door Tom caught her arm, holding it firmly. 'What's the rush? You were keen enough to stay a moment ago.'

'Oh! How could you!' Jenna tried to shake her arm free but it was held in an iron grip. 'You took advantage of me!' Her words, said in a low, trembling voice, sounded dramatic even to her, and she bit her lip. He would really be laughing at her in a moment.

'You are right. That was a rotten thing to say. Unforgivable.' Tom wasn't laughing, he spoke soberly. 'Look, you're overwrought. I'll walk you home.'

'I'll walk myself home, thank you very much. After all, it's just down the road!'

'Very well.' Tom shrugged.

'Goodnight,' snapped Jenna and hurried

off down the road, never noticing that he followed, keeping an eye on her until she slipped into the drive of her home.

The lights were out downstairs and Jenna crept in and up to her room, trying not to disturb the family. She undressed and washed her face and hands, scrubbing at her lips which looked swollen and red in the bathroom mirror. Tom had said he was interested in her; why had he treated her like that? Jenna climbed into bed and lay there, her mind in a whirl. She could still feel his arms around her, his hands on her body; surely she couldn't have imagined the strength of his response; surely it had been as great as hers? She remembered the hardness of his body against hers, the intoxicating scent of his masculinity. Yet he had put her away from him; she would have done anything for him, given him anything.

'I must have been out of my senses!' Jenna said aloud, burning with humiliation. He had kissed her out of temper, that was all, because she had annoyed him; he meant it as some sort of punishment. And she, fool that she was, had surprised and embarrassed him by the strength of her response, so he had stopped. Jenna squirmed at the very thought. It was as she had always supposed, he was not really interested in her as a woman, but as her father's daughter. As soon as he had finished his appointment at the hospital he would be gone without a backward glance at her.

'He won't catch me like that again,' she vowed. 'My guard will be up all the time. Diane is welcome to him, she wants him all right.' Jenna realized she was mumbling into her pillow and resolutely put all thoughts of Tom and the wretched Diane out of her mind, determined to sleep.

Just then she heard the telephone ring, insistent with its penetrating buzz, and her father's voice as he picked up the extension receiver by the bedside. He listened, then spoke in answer and Jenna realized he was quietly dressing and getting ready to go out. Emergency at the hospital, she surmised; it must be bad for it was not often David was called out even when the registrar was off duty. She speculated no further, after all she was a doctor's daughter, such happenings were part of family life. But the incident had succeeded in taking her mind off her own troubles and she dropped into a deep, refreshing sleep.

Jenna usually slept in a little the morning after her first night off, so she was surprised when she woke and glancing at her watch saw it was only half-past seven. Stretching luxuriously she turned over onto her back and pulled the duvet up under her chin. No rush this morning, she thought. But something must have wakened her; lazily her mind searched for what it was that was different in the early-morning, familiar sounds of the house.

That was it, she realized suddenly, someone was talking in the hall, a man's voice, not her father's; it was Tom. Now what on earth did he want at this time of the morning? A feeling of unease made her reach for her warm dressing-gown and slippers. Combing her hair with her fingers as she went, she reached the stairs and looked down into the hall to see Tom and Pam just going through to the lounge.

'Don't worry, Pam, he will be all right,' Tom was saying as Jenna ran down the stairs, alarm rising in her. 'I came to tell you myself, David thought it would be better. I'll take you to the hospital now if—'

'What's wrong? What happened?' Jenna's apprehensive voice broke in. Tom and Pam both turned towards the door, Pam's usually sunny face dark and distressed. She sank down on a chair wordlessly. Tom glanced at her quickly then went to Jenna

'Come in and sit down, Jenna.'

'It's father!' Something dreadful had happened to her father, she knew it. She stared up at him, her eyes black pools in her white face.

'He's going to be all right.' Tom took her arm firmly and guided her to a chair. 'David was called out during the night, a road traffic accident, a boy with a ruptured spleen.' He stopped and stared at Jenna, his expression unreadable.

'But what happened? Did Daddy have an accident?'

Tom walked over to Pam and put his hand on her shoulder.

'It was that gang. They were fighting in the middle of the road, out of their minds with drink and God knows what else; one of them drove a motor-bike into the middle of them. Hence the lad with the ruptured spleen. The others were only cuts and bruises, but they were in casualty. Causing a rumpus. David was passing and went to the aid of the nurses. One of them pulled a knife. David was stabbed.'

Pam gave a stifled sob, and Tom stopped speaking and squeezed her shoulder. Jenna waited dumbly for him to go on, wanting to hear the worst and yet not wanting to.

'As I said, he will be all right. Thank God, the knife missed any vital organ.'

'I'll have to go to him,' Pam said. 'I would have gone sooner; why weren't we told sooner?' She had stopped crying and blew her nose.

'David didn't want you to be alarmed by a phone call in the middle of the night. We got him straight to theatre and there was no point in telling you immediately. In any case, he wanted me to tell you.'

Pam nodded, it was like David to be so considerate even when he was hurt. 'I'll go and get ready; you'll see to Annie?' she enquired of Jenna.

'Yes, of course.'

'I'll run you down,' said Tom. 'I must go back to check on things. Thank goodness they rang me last night on the off chance I was home.'

Jenna was still sitting staring at Tom, her nerves tingling with shock. He waited until

Pam was out of the room before turning to her.

'What gang?' she asked, though in the back of her mind she knew.

'What gang indeed,' he said coldly. 'Who but your precious Wayne Johns and his mates? Now do you realize what you were messing about with, you little fool?'

Jenna was stunned by the cruelty of it, she stared up at him uncomprehendingly. Did he think it was somehow her fault?

'I—I—Are you blaming me for this?' She found her voice at last. 'Are you saying it's because of me?'

'Hospital drugs were found in John's possession; the police say so. I didn't want to say in front of Pam but there will be an investigation.'

'And you think it was me?' Jenna was incredulous; how could he possibly think that?

'I don't know who the culprit is, but you can rest assured we will find out.'

'And you will find out I had nothing to do with it!' said Jenna furiously. 'I have no access to the drug cupboard; have you forgotten I'm still in training? Only trained nurses have access. And everything is double checked!' She choked suddenly, and struggled to gain control. 'How could you think I would—'

'Everyone who was acquainted with Johns and his lot will be questioned. And you—'

He was interrupted by the sound of Pam running down the stairs. 'I'm ready, Tom,' she said. She had calmed herself and was composed though pale. 'Jenna, Annie is awake now. It's her nursery-school day, so you will be able to come down to the hospital as soon as you've got her there. Sure you don't mind?'

'Of course not.' Jenna's feelings were in turmoil, but she managed to smile a little at her stepmother. 'I'm sure he'll be all right, Pam.'

'Yes,' said Tom. 'Shall we go then?' He

took Pam's arm gently and led her out to the car.

Jenna was left standing in the hall staring at the closed door after they had gone. Now she was on her own, she relaxed her hold on herself, bowing her head she let the tears flow. But even now she only had a few moments, Annie had been talking happily to her doll in her cot, but now she began to sound impatient, crying out for attention.

'Just a minute, love!' Jenna called and quickly blew her nose. Annie's face was puckering as she started to give a demanding wail, but it swiftly turned into a sunny smile as she saw Jenna come into the room.

'Come on, darling, time for breakfast!' Jenna slid down the side of the cot and Annie scrambled out. She was getting to the age where she liked to do everything herself; soon she would need a bed, thought Jenna, before she tried climbing out on her own.

'Where's Mummy?' the child demanded as Jenna was getting her cereal and milk in the kitchen.

'She had to go out, love.' Jenna poured herself a cup of coffee from the still warm coffee-pot which Pam had left. Annie didn't make a fuss, she was as happy with Jenna as she was with her parents. She began making patterns in her cereal with her spoon.

'Hurry up, Annie, you have to go to school, we are going to walk there today.'

All the time Jenna was seeing to the child, getting her ready to go out and face the cold, changing herself into pants and a sweater covered by a thick windcheater, she was deliberately pushing all thoughts of anything else to the back of her mind. But when she had left Annie at the nursery and was hurrying on to the hospital, walking into a bitter north-east wind which whipped bright colour into her cheeks, her thoughts were chaotic.

Worry about her father was uppermost

in her mind; had Tom deliberately under-played his injury? How could David have been stabbed and it not be serious? How could a surgeon be stabbed in his own hospital in a sleepy little town like Darnton? But Tom wouldn't have said he was in no danger unless it was true, she reminded herself. But then her thoughts turned back to Tom, his hurtful words burning into her; never would she forget the sight of his blue eyes blazing with contempt, his mouth taut and white under his tan. He really had thought she was capable of procuring drugs, yet she had never given him reason to doubt her character. How could he?

She was entering the hospital gates now; she hurried up the drive and round to the surgical side feeling desperately unreal, the familiar corridors and wards seeming so different to when she was dressed in her nurse's uniform, ready to do her duty for other people, other patients. Now she was on the other side of the fence and she knew how relatives of patients must be feeling.

David was in a private ward, as of course she knew he would be. He was propped on one side with the aid of pillows and Pam was sitting by his side, holding his hand tightly. Jenna felt an intruder as she knocked and opened the door, they looked so involved with each other, but they looked up as she went in.

'Hi there, Jenna!' David smiled up at his daughter, and his voice sounded quite firm. 'Isn't this a nice pickle I got myself into?' Even as she grinned in reply she was noting the bandage around his chest and over his shoulder. He looked tired and pale, but she could see that Tom was right, he was going to be OK.

'Oh, Daddy!' she said weakly, and leaned against the wall. Suddenly her legs felt rather wobbly.

'You'd better sit down.' David had seen her change of colour and glanced quickly at Pam who drew up another chair for Jenna and waved her into it. They watched her for a moment in some concern.

'It's all right, Jenna really,' said Pam. 'The knife was in the back, but it was deflected by the scapula and the wound isn't deep. But the deflection caused it to tear the muscle and he lost a bit of blood. But he's going to be fine.' She took hold of David's hand again as though she couldn't bear for them not to be touching, and smiled lovingly at him.

There was a knock at the door and Sister appeared.

'Excuse me, Mr Neville, Mrs Neville,' she said, and looked at Jenna. 'Can I see you for a moment, Nurse Neville?' she said formally.

'Yes, of course.' Jenna stood and followed her out to the corridor.

'The police would like a word with you,' said Sister. 'They are in the office.'

Nine

Jenna knocked on the door of the office with some trepidation. She knew she had done nothing wrong, but those few seconds as she knocked and obeyed the command to enter were the worst she had endured in her whole life.

Suppose they didn't believe in her innocence? What would it do to her father, the family who loved her? In this town where they lived, where they were respected and where she had lived since she was born, where everyone knew them, the disgrace would be terrible! Her heart was hammering against her ribs and her mouth and throat went dry with tension, as she faced the men in the room, a young police constable and Inspector James, a friend of her father's. Dear God, she thought in a panic, why did it have to be Inspector James?

'Gracious, Nurse Neville,' exclaimed the grey-haired inspector as he rose from the desk to greet her. 'There's no need to look so frightened, I'm not going to eat you! You look like a frightened rabbit facing a fox! Come and sit down, I only want to ask you a few questions.'

'Questions?'

Jenna's voice croaked in her dry throat and she swallowed nervously.

'That's right.' The inspector indicated a chair he had drawn up to the desk. 'Do sit down, Jenna.' His manner had changed slightly from when she came in and he had addressed her so formally. Now he was obviously trying to put her at her ease. She slipped into the chair and clasped her hands together to stop them shaking.

'What would you like to know, inspector?' she said, and was pleased to hear her voice sounded almost normal.

'I understand that you were at school

with these young hooligans and were still on speaking terms with one of them at least? I mean Wayne Johns?'

'Yes.'

'Yes, well, I don't know if you are aware that they were not only drunk last night, but they had broken into the pharmacy looking for drugs.'

'The pharmacy?' Surprise was evident in Jenna's face and Inspector James paused and looked at her keenly before continuing.

'Fortunately, they did not manage to reach the dangerous drugs, no doubt you are aware that is practically impossible. In fact we are surprised they managed to get as far as they did without being caught. They must have known the lay-out of the place very well. Perhaps even had inside help.'

What was he getting at, Jenna wondered, slightly mystified; she couldn't have helped them there, the only part of the pharmacy she had any knowledge of was the hatch where she sometimes had to pick up something needed for a patient in a hurry.

'What has this to do with me, inspector?' she asked at last, feeling somehow much better now she knew she wasn't suspected of giving them drugs from the ward.

'Just an off chance, Jenna. I thought as you knew him, well, it occurred to me that he might have mentioned being friendly with someone employed in the pharmacy?'

'No, inspector. Wayne never mentioned anything like that; as far as I know he didn't know anyone else in the hospital. But of course, he's lived in the town all his life, he could know loads of people.'

'Yes, of course.' The inspector looked down at his papers, his forehead creased in thought. Jenna waited patiently to see if he wanted to know any more from her. The policeman sitting by the door making notes coughed and crossed his legs, breaking the silence.

'Is that all, inspector?' Jenna ventured at last.

'What?' The inspector gave her a quick glance and stood up, holding out his hand to her. 'Oh, yes, sorry, I was thinking. Yes, of course you can get back to your father, and tell him I hope he'll soon be fit enough to go round the golf course with me.'

A feeling of relief washed over Jenna, she could hardly believe it was over. 'Thank you, inspector,' she heard herself say, as she escaped into the corridor. She leaned against the wall for a moment to collect herself, before returning to her father's bedside. As she opened the door Pam swiftly put her finger to her lips. David was asleep, sleeping deeply and evenly. Pam picked up her bag and they went quietly out.

'What did the police want with you?' enquired Pam as they went out of the ward for a few minutes' fresh air.

'Nothing much. They knew I knew Wayne, and thought I might know of anyone he knew in pharmacy who might have helped him break in. But I didn't.'

'They think someone in the hospital helped him?' Pam sounded surprised. 'Surely that's unlikely! It would be more than anyone's job was worth.'

Jenna shrugged. 'I couldn't help them anyway.' They walked up the path a little way then turned back. It was too cold to stay out long, so they soon went back into the ward, where they found David still asleep.

'Do you want me to pick up Annie from the nursery? I could, easily, if you like,' offered Jenna. It was almost twelve o'clock.

Pam peeped in at David. 'Thanks Jenna but I don't think I'll stay. We may as well both go and collect her. I'll just have a word with Sister.'

Sister agreed they might as well go home as David was asleep and in no danger. 'Dr Yorke said I'd to let him know when you were ready to go and he would give you a lift as you haven't got your car,' she said to Pam and lifted the receiver.

'Oh, don't bother,' said Pam much to Jenna's relief. 'The walk won't hurt us, eh, Jenna?'

So they collected Annie, who was proudly holding a picture she had coloured. Jenna felt slightly unreal as they sat in the kitchen eating lunch, with Annie chattering away about her picture and her friend at the nursery. Pam answered her mechanically; she looked tired and still a little anxious as though she couldn't quite believe that David was really going to be all right.

'Why don't you lie down for half an hour, then go back in to Daddy?' suggested Jenna. 'I can easily see to Annie.'

'Oh, would you?' Pam was grateful. 'I feel I want to go straight back in, just to make sure there was no mistake and he is OK.'

'Go on then. Since Annie is so fond of colouring, we'll do some more this afternoon.'

Pam had driven off in her little car

and Jenna was sitting at the kitchen table with Annie. The table was covered with paint-sticks and paper. Jenna was drawing animals, to Annie's orders, and Annie was colouring them carefully, doing surprisingly well for a two-year-old, when the doorbell rang.

'Here you are then, an elephant,' said Jenna handing over a rather peculiar drawing of an elephant, before answering the door. Standing there, seeming to fill the whole entrance, was Tom.

'Aren't you going to ask me in?' he said coolly, as she glared at him without speaking. Not trusting herself to speak she stood aside and he walked past into the hall.

'We're in the kitchen,' she snapped at last and banging the door she marched through, leaving him to follow or not. Annie looked up at Tom and gave him a cherubic smile; she was a friendly little soul and loved visitors.

'Elethump,' she said helpfully, and

proudly showed him a bright red and yellow work of art.

'Very nice, Annie!' he said admiringly, then turned to Jenna. 'Any chance of a cup of coffee?' For all the world as though they never had a cross word, she thought with some heat; nevertheless, she switched the kettle on to boil and spooned instant coffee into two mugs.

'I don't know how you have the nerve to come here after accusing me of such things.' She spoke in a conversational tone, not wishing to upset Annie.

'I brought David's car back,' he said mildly. 'He will be in hospital a day or two, best not to leave it there. I guessed you and Pam must have forgotten all about it.'

'Thank you.' The words of thanks were almost forced out of her, before she returned to the attack. 'I thought you might want to apologize for what you said to me this morning. You must have known then that I had nothing to do with it, yet you let me think I was suspect.'

In spite of the need not to upset Annie her voice rose slightly, ending in a slight squeak as she tried to keep it down. She was trembling with anger.

'I didn't actually say that,' said Tom, smiling at Annie and offering her a brown paint-stick. 'Try this colour, Annie.'

Annie took the stick and bent her head over a drawing of a tiger, completely absorbed.

'You implied it!'

Tom caught Jenna's eye and considered her flushed face, the trembling lip. His expression changed, something flickering at the back of his eyes, his sculptured mouth softened.

'Look, Jenna, I'm sorry. Is that what you want me to say? I shouldn't have gone on at you, especially when you had had such a shock. Truce?' He smiled at her, his eyes lighting up, his mouth lifting at one corner. He stretched a hand over the table and covered hers, his fingers warm and steady over her own. She looked down at his hand, feeling her anger dissolving, melting away beneath his gaze. Which was all very well, but she sensed the apology was not really heartfelt; he was using his undoubted charm on her and what was more it was working.

'But—' she began, with a last flicker of resentment.

'Come on, Jenna. Truce? I was angry because I was worried about you.' He turned her hand over and stroked the palm.

'Let's start again, Jenna?' His voice was low and intimate, his thumb was sending tremors of feeling up her arm. She looked up into his eyes, those deep, deep eyes, so deep blue she was drowning in them. His thumb covered the pulse at her wrist and lingered there, and his smile deepened. Jenna knew he had noted the race of her heartbeat and was drawing his own conclusions, but she was helplessly entangled, bewitched and bewildered as the old song said.

'Finished, Jenna. Look what I did!' It was the persistent voice of Annie which brought Jenna back to reality, like a douche of cold water. Quickly she snatched her hand away, her face burning, then turned to the child who was holding out her picture. She was glad to turn away from Tom, and exclaimed with wonder over the drawing, giving it all her attention while she fought to gain control over her wildly beating heart, her trembling fingers.

'See, darling,' she said when she could trust herself to speak. 'I'll get the bluetack and we will fasten the pictures on the wall. Won't that be a nice surprise when Mummy gets home?'

Tom sat back in his chair, a half smile on his face, his long legs stretched under the table. Lazily he watched them sticking up the brightly-coloured drawings; Jenna could feel his eyes on her back but she resolutely kept her mind on Annie and the pieces of paper and bluetack.

'There now!' she said at last, as they

stood back to survey their handiwork. 'Now it's time for your nap.' Annie made little protest, she was already beginning to yawn.

'I'll have to take Annie up now,' Jenna said to Tom, rather formally. 'You can let yourself out if you like.'

'Oh, don't worry about me,' he answered. 'I'll just sit here and wait. I'm in no hurry.'

'Don't you have to get back then?'

'Not this afternoon, I'm free; if I'm wanted urgently they know where I am.' He was imperturbable. Jenna could think of nothing to say, so she gathered Annie up in her arms and took her upstairs.

Annie went quietly, her eyes already closing as Jenna laid her down, so Jenna took the opportunity to slip into the bathroom to splash her face with cold water. She dragged a comb through her hair, smoothing its heaviness away from her face and fastening it simply with a slide. Staring into the mirror, she studied

211

the face looking back at her; her nose was too snub, she decided, it was a perfectly ordinary face if she got rid of the bemused expression in the dark eyes. Not at all a beauty, not at all to be compared with the golden-haired Diane.

Jenna shook herself mentally, allowing herself a wry grin in the mirror. What on earth did it matter after all, she had no intention of competing with Diane? It wouldn't do her any good if she did. She would go downstairs and be normal and polite with Tom and nothing more.

'You're still here!' she commented rather obviously as she went back into the kitchen. She began clearing away the paper and paint-sticks, clearing the table. Tom watched her patiently until the kitchen was tidied to her satisfaction and she couldn't think of anything else to do.

'Finished?' he said at last. 'Right then, sit down.' Jenna found herself obediently sitting down beside him.

'You didn't answer me,' said Tom.

'What about?'

'I asked you if we had a truce.' Tom leaned across and lifted her chin with one finger, forcing her to look into his eyes.

'Truce,' she said. A warm glow was spreading from where his finger had contact with the soft skin of her chin. After all, what was the use of fighting?

Tom bent his head and studied her softly parted lips, rosy without the aid of lip-gloss. She felt the beginning of that excitement which was now becoming only too familiar. His gaze was so intense as he slowly lowered his head and kissed her, gently at first, softly tasting her lips. Her eyes closed as she gave herself up to the delight of the feelings his kisses were arousing in her. Then they flew open, almost in protest, as he lifted his head for a moment. His eyes, darkened almost to navy-blue, looked into the dark brown of hers.

The pause was only momentary, Tom must have seen what he wanted to see, for he kissed her again, not questioning this time, but a masterful, almost triumphant kiss, which seemed to singe her mouth, taking her breath.

'Jenna,' he said softly at last. 'Jenna, you are enough to drive a man crazy! This is no time to start anything.' He released her and sat up straight in his chair. 'I think I'd better go, while I still retain some common sense!'

Tom stood up and ran his fingers through his hair. Unspeaking, Jenna looked up at him. For the first time she thought he might love her. How could he kiss her like that and raise such a response in her if he didn't love her? So what did he mean by saying he didn't want to start anything?

The spell was broken by the insistent ring of the telephone. Jenna walked over to the extension on the kitchen wall and picked it up, still looking at Tom.

'Hello? Is that the Nevilles' house? I understand Dr Yorke is there.' The voice paused and waited for Jenna's affirmative,

Diane's voice. 'Well, can I speak to him?' The tone of the voice sharpened.

Jenna held out the receiver to Tom without speaking. She walked out of the kitchen and into the lounge, feeling curiously let down. This was really the answer to the questions she had been asking herself a moment ago. Tom didn't want to start anything with her because of the lovely Diane. The phone had rang just in time to stop her making a fool of herself. She could hear Tom's voice in the background, but not what he was saying.

Angrily she began laying the log fire in the hearth ready for the evening; it hadn't been lit all day as Pam was at the hospital.

'Jenna?'

Tom was standing in the doorway, his mood completely changed. 'I've got to go now,' he said briskly. 'Diane is bringing my car out for me.' He leaned on the door jamb whistling softly to himself and watching Jenna absently.

Obviously his mind was miles away,

thought Jenna crossly; the fair Diane only had to ring and she herself was completely forgotten. She couldn't resist saying rather bitterly, 'Oh yes, Diane of course.'

Tom stopped whistling and looked at her with raised eyebrows. Furiously, she realized she had given herself away and tried to cover it up by attacking the hearth with a vigorous brush, sweeping imaginary ashes into the well of the fire.

'You're not jealous; of course you're not.' There was a definite note of laughter in Tom's voice.

'Why should I be jealous?' Jenna was pleased to hear her voice sounded firm and unemotional. She even straightened up and looked him in the eye. Luckily at that moment there was the sound of a car in the drive.

'That must be her now. Don't keep her waiting on my account,' she continued sweetly.

He looked undecided for a second, then turned on his heel and went out without a retort. Score to me, thought Jenna savagely. She listened to the sound of the car driving away and fading into the distance before flinging herself onto the settee. She was thoroughly out of humour. Why on earth did she let herself be conned by Tom Yorke? It was so obvious that he was simply making use of her, and what was worse he knew the effect he had on her and manipulated her accordingly. But Diane only had to come back into the picture and she, Jenna was forgotten. Well, she decided angrily, he wouldn't get the chance to do it again, she was going to keep up her guard, she could be as hard as he was.

By the time Pam came home she had the fire going, supplementing the central heating; the lounge was vacuumed and dusted even though Mrs Evans, the home help, came next day; and there was a delicious casserole simmering in the oven.

'Gosh, that smells heavenly!' Pam sank down in her chair by the fire and kicked off her shoes, stretching her toes to the fire. 'Ooh, lovely and warm.'

'It's lamb casserole,' said Jenna 'I hunted around in the freezer. How's Dad then, I gather he's all right?'

'Yes. He'll be coming home tomorrow,' Pam said. 'Thank God it was no worse. But he does look tired and worn. I've persuaded him to take some time off; in any case he can't work until he is completely recovered.' She lay back in her chair and Annie, who had been playing quietly with her dolls, clambered up onto her lap. Pam rubbed her cheek against the soft fair head. She too looked tired and worn, the aftermath of the shock, thought Jenna.

'Dr Yorke brought Dad's car back,' volunteered Jenna.

'Oh yes. That was good of him. Did he stay long?'

'Not long,' said Jenna thinly. 'Diane Woodford came for him with his own car.'

Pam looked at her closely. 'Diane

Woodford? Do I know her?'

'She's Charlie Stelling's cousin. A blonde woman, with a cultivated tan, you may have met her.'

'Oh yes. She's doing research at Durham University. Her parents have a boarding-house or hotel in Devon somewhere. They moved down there years ago when he was made redundant.'

Jenna stared at Pam mystified. She really was a mine of information, she knew everyone in the town.

'How did you know that?'

'Oh well, my mother happened to mention it last time I was over there. Evidently she knew them years ago.' Pam lay back against the cushions and gazed into the fire as though the effort of talking had tired her.

'Look, Pam.' Jenna watched her with some concern. 'I will go in to see Dad on my own tonight. You still seem a bit shaken, why don't you have an early night? We know Dad's going to be OK.'

'It means you walking in or going on the bus,' Pam objected. 'If only you would take your test, you could have used my car.'

'I know. But I don't mind. Anyway, you know I decided to get my finals over with first. One test at a time, that's my motto.'

Jenna caught the bus into town to see David, so she was in good time for visiting hours, though as staff at the hospital they could come and go more or less as they wished. As she opened the door to the side ward she was pleased to see he was sitting up in bed looking a great deal better than he had that morning. He seemed rested and cheerful, putting down his book and giving her a welcoming smile as she came in and sat down after kissing him on the cheek.

'How do you like being a patient for a change then, Dad?'

'Not a lot. I'll have a bit more sympathy for the poor souls under my care after this,' David twinkled.

'I bet you're running the poor nurses ragged too,' Jenna laughed. 'Doctors make absolutely the very worst patients.'

David put on a mock-dignified expression. 'Not at all. I'm a model of quiet, suffering patience,' he said. 'Isn't that right, Sister?' Day Sister had opened the door behind Jenna and father and daughter looked up at her, laughing.

'I wouldn't exactly say that,' she temporized. 'I've brought your medication, Mr Neville.' She held out a medicine glass containing capsules. David frowned slightly. It was obviously in his mind to question them.

'Now, father,' said Jenna gently, 'you're a model patient, remember?'

David sighed. 'Oh, righto, I know,' he said resignedly. Obediently he took the capsules and drank some water.

'There's a good boy,' murmured Sister wickedly, and winked at Jenna before going out.

'I won't stay long. If you get a good

221

night's sleep you will be home all the sooner.' Jenna smiled fondly at him. To be honest she felt worn out herself, the events of the morning had taken their toll of her stamina too. David noted the dark shadows under her eyes, the weariness which was beginning to show in her face.

'That's a good idea,' he said. 'You get off home to bed, I won't be long before I'm asleep myself. How are you getting home?'

'I'll get the bus. It's due in five minutes.'

'Are you sure? Tom will be off in a minute, I'm sure he would run you back.' David was a little bothered about her travelling at night on the bus.

'No, no, it's not far. I'll have to run now though.' Hurriedly Jenna kissed him goodnight and rushed out, before he could insist on contacting Tom Yorke. Luckily, a bus was coming along as she reached the stop and she climbed on thankfully. She really couldn't bear meeting up with Tom again that night.

Ten

David was soon well enough to come home, but he wasn't considered well enough to take up his duties at the hospital for a while. His wound had healed up nicely, but he was sufficiently shaken by the incident to realize he needed to get away for a few weeks.

Wayne and his friends were scheduled to go to trial in the new year, so there was nothing to stop David and Pam from taking Annie and going to the South of France for a month to soak up the sunshine and complete David's recovery.

'You don't mind, do you, Jenna?' Pam asked her step-daughter. 'If you don't want to stay in the house alone you will probably be able to move into the nurses' home while we are away.'

'Oh no, I'll be quite all right,' Jenna reassured her. 'It'll be nice and quiet and I'll get on with revising. There's no need to go into the nurses' home.'

So it was arranged; anything urgent on David's list was attended to by the other surgical consultants who divided the work between them, and soon Jenna was seeing her family off at Newcastle airport.

Tom had actually driven David's car up to the airport and handled the luggage for the little family. It was the first time Jenna had seen him except for the formal meetings in the hospital where their relationship had been strictly in the context of doctor and nurse.

Now, as they went back out to the car, Jenna felt strangely shy, feeling she must have given away how she felt about him that afternoon when he brought back her father's car.

Tom settled her courteously in the passenger seat before climbing in himself. But he didn't drive away immediately, he sat watching her gravely, until at last she felt compelled to meet his eyes.

'Hello, my little Jenna,' he said softly. Then, leaning over to her, he brushed his lips gently over hers, feeling them quiver in response. He picked up a lock of her glossy brown hair which was curling over her shoulder, and smoothed it between finger and thumb. In spite of herself Jenna couldn't stop the rising tide of yearning attraction which threatened to take over her treacherous body.

Tom smiled slightly, with a hint of triumph, and his kiss was insistent this time; his hand dropped to cup her small well-shaped breast through her fine lambswool sweater. Even through the wool her nipple hardened at the rhythmic stroke of his thumb.

'No!'

Somehow Jenna managed to summon the strength to wrench away from his grasp, moving as far away from him as she possibly could within the confines of the car.

'No?'

Tom was looking down at her with a quizzical gaze, one corner of his mouth turned up slightly and laughter in his deep blue eyes.

Jenna was shaking with the depth of feeling generated by his caress and the effort she had needed to pull away from him.

'Why not?' he insisted. 'You don't deny your feelings for me, surely?' He picked up her hand and ran his fingers up the palm until he reached the thudding pulse at her wrist. Anger came to Jenna's rescue.

'You think you only have to kiss a girl and she's yours!' she burst out hotly. 'Well, you've picked on the wrong girl! Diane's more your type anyway!'

Tom released his hold of her wrist and fastened his seat-belt. He was smiling openly now and Jenna was furious with herself for mentioning Diane; he was bound to think she was jealous now, it would make him even more insufferable!

'Just as you like,' Tom said mildly, however, as he eased the car out of the car-park and turned it onto the road south.

They spoke little on the journey; he concentrated on the motorway traffic and she concentrated on getting her feelings under control. She was absolutely determined to be coolly calm with him in the future; she would wipe the amusement from his eyes!

They had been travelling fairly fast on the motorway, but as they left it Tom slowed to meet the different conditions of the stretch of two-way country road which led back to the little town of Darnton. Which was just as well, for rounding a broad bend they were confronted by a man jumping up and down in the middle of the road and waving his arms up and down frantically.

Tom pulled the car over onto the grass

verge and rolled down his window as the man ran to him, the relief of actually getting someone to stop evident in his face.

'Thank God, man! I thought no-one was going to stop! I—we need help. My wife's having a baby and I've run the car off the road!'

Tom wasted no time in asking for more information but quickly got out of the car and set off after the frantic husband with Jenna not far behind him.

'Where is it?' he asked as they hurried round the bend, but before the man could answer they came upon the crashed car. It was an old red Fiesta, lying half in the ditch, with the front resting against a telegraph pole, the red metal bent and twisted. By the side of the car lay a woman, writhing in pain, and beside her, weeping silently, stood a little boy.

'Jimmy!' cried Jenna in astonishment. It was Jimmy Stephenson. Jenna remembered him from her days in casualty when he came in with a broken arm.

'Come on, Jimmy, come away for a minute, your mam will be all right, the doctor's here.' Jenna's training took over and she led the little boy to the back of the car.

'A doctor? That right, he's a doctor?' Mr Stephenson's face lightened with hope.

Tom was leaning over Mrs Stephenson, feeling her body gently, looking for injuries. 'Why did you move her; don't you know it could have been dangerous?' he said tersely.

'But I didn't, she climbed out herself; I was knocked out for a moment. When I came to, she and Jimmy were out of the car. Then she just collapsed, and I saw the baby was coming, it must have been the shock.' He was staring down at his wife, his own face white and strained except for a purpling bruise which was rising on one temple.

'A car came round the bend on the wrong side of the road and I had to swerve,' he said, wonderingly. 'The beggar didn't even stop to see if anyone was hurt!'

Tom looked at him keenly. It was obvious he needed to do something or he too would collapse.

'Go and try to flag down another car; get them to ring the police and an ambulance. Hurry now!' He spoke sharply. Mr Stephenson must keep himself alert until the emergency services arrived. 'Take Jimmy with you!' He called as an afterthought, 'We'll see to your wife!'

Once Jimmy and his father had gone Jenna came and knelt at the other side of the labouring woman. Though not trained in midwifery, she had done a session on Maternity, and it was obvious to her that the birth of the baby was imminent. Mrs Stephenson was drawing up her knees convulsively and moaning quietly; Tom had taken off his sheepskin jacket to cover her but she was shivering with the cold.

'I'll run back and get the rug out of

the car,' offered Jenna and Tom nodded without looking up. Even as Jenna ran back to their own car she was marvelling at the way he had sized up the situation and was taking charge with such calm and expertise.

Thank goodness her father kept such a warm, fleecy rug in the car, she had time to think, as she grabbed it and set off back at a run. Out of the corner of her eye she noticed that Mr Stephenson had managed to stop a car and was talking swiftly to the driver. So at least it would not be too long before the arrival of the emergency services.

'Someone has gone for the police and ambulance,' she commented as she knelt by Mrs Stephenson with the rug.

'Good.' Tom didn't look up, he was timing the labour pains. 'Only two minutes there. And getting closer all the time. Let's hope the ambulance gets here in time, it's very cold out here to deliver a baby.'

As it happened, though the ambulance

was there within ten minutes, the tiny girl had already made her entrance into the world, assisted by Tom and quickly wrapped in Jenna's warm anorak. Then suddenly all was hustle and bustle as the ambulance crew arrived, and mother and child were soon ensconced in the warm ambulance, with Tom checking that everything else could safely wait until arrival at the hospital.

Jenna picked up the rug and Tom's discarded jacket as she waited for him. Glancing round she noticed the white-faced father, clutching little Jimmy to him, swaying slightly and shivering violently in the bitter wind.

'Can Mr Stephenson and the boy come in now?' she called to Tom, as he straightened up from the stretcher.

'Better help them, there's no reason why they can't come in the ambulance.' He nodded to the paramedic. 'Right, I'll leave you to it now.'

The ambulance pulled away, leaving

them standing on the verge. The wind was biting cold, but both Jenna and Tom felt a sense of warm satisfaction.

'Better get off now, sir, before you catch pneumonia.' The policeman near them turned up his overcoat collar against the wind. 'Shouldn't be surprised if we have snow before the night's out.' He surveyed the car crashed against the telegraph pole. 'Jolly good thing you happened along, sir. Well, we can get in touch with you at the hospital then.'

It was sheer delight to get back into the warmth of the car, away from the wind. They sat in a companionable silence as Tom drove home and put the car away in David's garage.

'Would you like to come in for some lunch?' Jenna felt it was the least she could offer. 'I can rustle up some ham and eggs.'

Tom studied her for a moment, she seemed tired, there were dark circles under her eyes.

'You're on duty tonight, aren't you?' he asked. 'I think I'd better go and let you get to bed. Unless you would like me to get *you* something, you look exhausted.'

'I think I'll go straight to bed.' Tom's words had had the effect of making her feel plain and unattractive, she really did need to get some sleep. She stood in the doorway, key in hand, watching him.

Tom smiled suddenly and bounded up the step to her. Stooping, he kissed her gently on the lips and taking the key from her opened the door and gave her a little shove inside.

'Go on,' he said. 'Go to bed. You look at me much longer with those appealing brown eyes and I won't be responsible. I'll see you tonight most likely.'

'Now what did he mean by that?' she wondered aloud as she watched him get into his MG, which had been parked on the drive, and take off.

Wearily she locked the door of the silent house and trailed upstairs to her bedroom.

She was too tired to think about it in any case; the most appealing place for her at the moment was bed.

Next morning, when Jenna had finished her period of ward duty, she decided to pay a visit to the maternity department to see Mrs Stephenson and her new baby. She felt slightly reluctant to go home, already she was missing the family. She walked along the path which connected the main hospital with the separate maternity blocks in the pale winter sunlight; the flower-beds looked bedraggled and forlorn, showing no hint of the spring blooms which would soon fill them with colour.

'We're quite busy, nurse.' Sister Maternity was slightly disapproving of such an early visitor. 'But you can go in for a few minutes.'

Mrs Stephenson was sitting up in bed looking pretty in a lacy bed-jacket and none the worse for the ordeal of the previous day. She was pleased to see

Jenna and proudly lifted up the baby for her to see.

'Oh, she's lovely,' exclaimed Jenna gazing at the little red-faced bundle with the silky mop of red-brown hair.

'Eight pounds,' said the fond mother, 'and the image of her dad!' She lay back on her pillow with the baby tucked into the crook of her arm. 'I'm so glad of the chance to thank you for what you did; goodness knows what I would have done if you hadn't stopped to help!'

'Well, I didn't do much,' Jenna said in deprecation. 'Really it was Dr Yorke who did everything.'

'He's your boyfriend, is he, nurse?'

'No!' Jenna's reply was quick, perhaps a little too quick. Mrs Stephenson smiled in a knowing way, head on one side.

'Maybe someday then,' she said, ignoring Jenna's vehement shake of the head.

'Someday indeed!'

Both women looked up at the sound of the deeply masculine voice, and Jenna flushed to see the laughter in Tom's eyes. He had entered the ward without their notice and was standing at the foot of the bed, looking fresh and handsome in his white coat, with the stethoscope dangling from his pocket.

'What are you doing here?' blurted Jenna.

'The same as you, I suppose.' Tom raised his eyebrows but his words were mild. 'I had a few minutes to spare so I thought I'd pay mother and child a little visit.' He transferred his attention to the baby held in Mrs Stephenson's arms. 'None the worse for greeting the world out in the cold, I see. A child to be proud of, Mrs Stephenson.'

'I'm so glad you came, doctor. I wanted to thank you again.' Mrs Stephenson was beaming with delight as she rocked the baby slightly against her breast.

'Well, I'll be going off home now.' Jenna was edging away from the bed. 'I must get some sleep.'

'Hang on a minute,' said Tom quickly. 'I'll walk along with you.'

They said their goodbyes and Jenna had perforce to go along with Tom, at least as far as the exit to the building. Tom opened the ward door for her, taking her arm and smiling down at her in such a way that her heart did a little jump.

'Hi there, Jenna! Dr Yorke!' Sally Spinks, the receptionist from casualty, was walking past, grinning cheerily at them, but with some speculation in her eyes.

'Oh Lord,' said Jenna 'The hospital grapevine is going to have a field day now. They'll have heard about the accident yesterday and they'll be wondering what we were doing together, and now—'

'So what!' The laughter had left Tom's face as he gave her an intent look. 'Why should it matter to us? Unless you're worried some boyfriend will get the wrong impression?'

Jenna was nonplussed for a second, his mood seemed to change so easily. 'Well, you know what it's like,' she faltered. Just then his bleeper sounded off, demanding attention.

'Blast the thing!' Tom took hold of her arm. 'Look, Jenna, I'm free on Monday and Tuesday; can you wangle your nights off to suit?'

'Why?'

'Because I have something very special to ask you. Come on, Jenna, tell me, I must go.'

Jenna thought rapidly, but the fact was that she knew she had to agree. She nodded, feeling puzzled. But Tom was already hurrying away, heading for the surgical unit, leaving her to stare after him. Perhaps he was interested in her, maybe even loved her. Sighing, she turned away. After all, there was Diane.

Eleven

Susan came back from Paris wearing an engagement ring and a seraphic smile. 'I wanted you to be the first to know.' She was sitting in the lounge with Jenna; she had an hour before she went on duty. Now she held out her hand to show off the pretty sapphire ring with its circlet of diamond chips.

'Of course, I know it's not expensive, but you know what junior doctors earn.'

'Yes of course, it's lovely. Oh Susan, I hope you'll be very happy.' Jenna hugged her friend. 'I'm sorry for what I said, Susan. I was wrong about Charlie.'

'Of course we won't be getting married straightaway. I'll finish my training and Charlie will finish his contract. Then he'll be seeking a post at a larger hospital in the south. Torbay perhaps.'

'What's wrong with here?' Jenna was moved to ask.

'Oh, Charlie thinks there will be more private patients in Devon. More money, you see. And of course he has relatives there. You've met his cousin, Diane. She's from there.'

Jenna stood up. She didn't want to be reminded of Diane. 'Time's getting on,' she reminded Susan, who scrambled to her feet.

'Heck yes, look at the time!' Susan was out of the door with a happy wave, and Jenna was left to wait for Tom.

She was ready and waiting when he finally arrived; the last couple of hours since Susan left had seemed like days to her. Her dark eyes were luminous in her slightly flushed face as she opened the door, causing him to catch his breath at the sight of her, her shining hair brushed loose over the shoulders of a rose-coloured sweater. She had pondered for ages over what to wear, but in the end decided on a simple straight skirt in dove-grey, and the rose-coloured sweater.

'Where are we going?' she asked, as she followed him to his car, the biting wind causing her to shiver suddenly.

'Cold, my love?' he murmured, and her eyes widened; surely she had misheard? The car was warm inside though, and Tom drove off into the night. 'We'll drive up Weardale.'

They stopped at a quiet pub high on the moor. The locals were gathered at one end of the bar in the single room; it was a large room with a blazing log fire at the other end and inglenook sofas drawn up beside it. It was almost like being in a room of their own.

They sat sipping their drinks, letting the warmth from the fire seep into their bones. Jenna was happy in a dreamlike way; she was not really much of a drinker and the brandy she was drinking combined with the heat of the fire made her drowsily content. Excitement welled up in her; her inhibitions lay dormant.

'Mmm ... nice,' she said and moved closer to Tom, slipping her hand into his and snuggling close.

'It is, isn't it?' Tom tipped her chin so that she was looking directly into his eyes, eyes which had darkened to midnight-blue.

As she watched, a muscle twitched at the side of his mouth; she studied it, fascinated. His strong, firm mouth, she thought; but her gaze was inevitably drawn to his eyes, she felt she would drown in their inky depths.

'If you look at me like that you can't expect me to be responsible for my actions.' Tom's voice was husky with desire; he ran his fingers up the inside of her arm, lightly, a feather touch, causing delicious tremors to her whole system. He laughed softly and sitting up straight, away from her, he took a sip from his glass.

Jenna felt a wave of yearning sweep over her as she watched him; long, muscular legs stretched out in front of him, the crisp, fair curls at the nape of his neck inviting her touch.

'I want to talk to you, Jenna to tell you my plans for the future,' Tom said at last.

'Yes?'

'You know I've been working for my Fellowship?'

'Your Fellowship? Yes, of course.' Jenna's immediate response was one of slight surprise; of course he would be working for his Fellowship, otherwise why would he be here?

'I've got it. That's where I was those few days I was away. Or didn't you miss me?' he added, a teasing grin on his face.

'Oh, congratulations! You kept that very quiet, didn't you? Now I'll have to call you Mr Yorke, I suppose!'

'Well, as a special concession you can call me Tom.' Tom picked up her hand again and contemplated it thoughtfully as he spoke. 'Of course I would be staying out my term here anyway. But I had intended to try for a post in Exeter or Torbay after that. Now I don't know. I am considering getting married.' He raised his eyes to hers, a strange, guarded expression in them.

The shock to Jenna was like a douche of ice-cold water. She snatched her hand away from him and clutched her drink; her mind felt numb as she gazed unseeingly at the fire, at the drawn curtains at the window, at anything but Tom's face.

The door opened and a man came in dressed in a duffel coat and farming boots which were encrusted with snow. The wind billowed round him, bringing a swirl of snowflakes into the bar with him. He pushed his hood back from his head, revealing the weather-beaten face of a fell shepherd.

'Bit of a storm out there blew up,' he commented as he knocked the snow from his boots in the doorway, before moving to the bar.

Jenna watched and heard him, but it was as though she was dreaming, she didn't take in his words at all.

'And Diane?' At last she found the words. 'What about Diane?'

'For goodness sake, Jenna what are you talking about?' Tom frowned, an impatient note to his voice. 'Diane has been offered a post as lecturer at Durham University. She's perfectly happy here.'

'Oh.'

Jenna was drowning in a sea of misery. That was why he had changed his mind about seeking a post back in his home county of Devon. Diane had a career to consider too. She gazed intently at her glass, then took a quick gulp.

'Jenna.'

'Yes?' She couldn't hide her feelings as she met his eyes.

'Jenna, it's you I want to marry, not Diane.'

'Me?'

'Of course it's you, you goose!' His grin was a little rueful as he took her face in both hands and kissed the trembling lips. 'Why else would I have brought you up here?'

He didn't have to wait for her answer, it was in her eyes. They were lost to the rest of the room for a while.

'Excuse me, sir, do you have far to go tonight?'

The voice of the barman made them look up; he was hovering near, an anxious expression on his face.

'Darnton.'

'Darnton?' The barman whistled softly. 'Nay lad, that wouldn't be wise.'

'Why not?' Tom's surprise showed on his face.

'There's a reet storm out there. Practically a white-out. T'road to Stanhope's drifted up to the top of the snow-poles.'

'We can go the other way though, down into Egglestone?'

'I wouldn't try that.' The barman gave the statement some emphasis. 'That'll be the same an' all.'

'But the forecast didn't mention anything about this!' burst out Tom.

'Nay, well, them men often miss mentioning Bolihope Common,' the barman said gravely. 'It blows up sudden-like, tha knows.'

Tom rushed to the door to see for himself, Jenna following and wrapping her jacket tightly about her as they went into the night. The wind whipped up her skirt and icy needles of freezing snow stung her cheeks.

The road was obliterated; even the car was only a mound of snow.

'We'd better go in, before we catch our death.' Tom took her arm and led her back into the warmth.

'We have a spare room,' said the barman. 'We're used to having to put people up.'

Tom and Jenna gazed at each other. 'We'll take it,' he said.

This Large Print Book for the Partially sighted, who cannot read normal print, is published under the auspices of

THE ULVERSCROFT FOUNDATION

Other Dales Romance Titles In Large Print